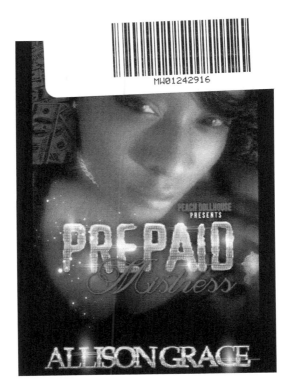

PEACH DOLLHOUSE
PRESENTS

PREPAID
Mistress

ALLISON GRACE

Acknowledgements

God is the beginning, middle and end of everything and without Him in my life, I don't know where I would be.

To my parents, I thank you for raising me to be someone that lives without regrets. Everything I've done is because I wanted to, good, bad & indifferent.

My sons, thank you for telling everyone that your mommy is famous. I'm not, but to know that I'm a celebrity in your eyes means so much to me and makes me seem invincible. I don't mind because my love for you lasts forever.

To those special friends that have TRULY supported me, I thank and love you! Y'all have been with me throughout the tears and the laughter. Thank you!

My author friends, I thank you all for standing by me and supporting my work. Kevon Gulley, Tamika Newhouse, Envy Red, Tanisha (Mahogani) Pettiford, Shonda DeVaughn, Mike O, Cha'Bella Don, Mimi Renee, Traci Bee, Charlene Braithwaite-Lovett, Julia Press Simmons, Eyone Williams, DC Bookdiva, Ashley & Jaquavis, Wahida Clark, K'wan, Treasure Blue and the entire Cash Money Content crew, Bella Jones, KD Harris, VJ Gotastory, Jason Poole, Charisse Washington, T. Styles and the rest of the Cartel Publications. I've learned so much from all of you and I thank you for the support you've given me. Love Ya!

Special shoutout to my publishers Sevyn McCray (I Love ya Pudd) & David Weaver for finding a diamond in the rough. This union is not by chance. I appreciate you all and the entire TBRS for the support and love. It's more than a label, it's a family! Extra special shout-out to my cover model Georgette Clark for the opportunity. I love you always!

To my fans and supporters within online book clubs, Twitter, Instagram, Facebook and beyond. Thank you for sticking with me and supporting my projects. I appreciate you all so very much. Your critique has made me better and I appreciate all the love you have given me. I can only get better with support from you. It's only the beginning of a journey that I plan to continue!

Whoever I "forgot", please know I love you still- Charge It To My Head and Not My Heart!

Much Love Always

Allison Grace

Enjoy other novels by

Allison Grace

Broken Promises Never Mend

Bound by Lies

Bittersweet

Christmas Kisses (a holiday short story)

All She Wants For Christmas is Love

(a holiday short story)

Prepaid Mistress 1 & 2

Bitch Clique Reloaded

Dedication

To the almighty dollar

there's nothing I couldn't do without you!

<u>Bad to the Bone</u>

The day my father died proved to me just how much my mother cared less of me and more of herself. She hated him but despised me because I favored him so much. Tears streamed down my face as I saw them put my daddy into the ground. The cold autumn wind whipped against my face. I heard the crackling beneath my feet as I stepped on dried leaves at the cemetery the day of his funeral a year ago. The dead leaves were a clear reflection of our relationship. It was once bright and flourishing but now it was dried and brittle. I will never forget that day nor how my mother looked at me when she heard the words he spoke declaring his love.

He said, "Coryn, you are the best thing that ever happened to me. I love you more than life itself." She glared at me with envy in her eyes as she watched our interaction. I knew I would eventually feel her wrath. I didn't know he would soon feel it too. I believed his feelings for me were true. He was my father and he was supposed to protect me.

I believed him until Momma found him with another woman.

My daddy loved me so much that he had another family. Mommy complained all the time about some whore taking most or all of his time. Here I was, eleven years old and with no daddy. I barely had a mother. She was so concentrated on my daddy that she neglected me. I often occupied myself with my dolls and with the neighbors next door. Mr. Tanner always made me feel better.

Momma was only worried about herself feeling better. She used the time she had and occupied herself with other men that made her feel better too. I thought about the last encounter I had with Mr. Tanner right before we left for the cemetery.

"Now there, there Coryn. Your mother is just inside talking to your neighbor. No need to be sad. I'm here to talk to you. If you like, we can play that game that we always play. I will let you win this time." Mr. Tanner reached into his pocket and pulled out a shiny silver dollar. I liked when he gave me money, but I hated what I had to do for it.

"Mr. Tanner, I don't wanna sit on your lap. It hurts my butt," I said staring up at him.

He let me into his apartment after he saw me sitting in the hallway reading. I loved reading. It was one of the only things that I could do for no one to bother me. I pretended to be the characters in the

3

books because they were living lives that I envied. I wanted to live in a big house with a dog and two parents that loved me. Hell, I even wanted a sibling that I could play with.

Sadly, my life was far from that. I lived with my mom and dad, who was out more than he was in. I spent a lot of time alone and hoping that my mom would stop drinking. I hated having to wake up and make my own lunch. The money I received from Mr. Tanner helped me buy cookies at school from the vending machine.

Mr. Tanner sat at his kitchen table and stared at his front door to see when and if my mother would be coming out soon. He picked me up and guided me to his lap. Instead of placing me on his knee, he had me sit directly in the middle which had a huge lump in the middle. I felt his penis caress my tiny mound and I gasped. I didn't want him to know I was nervous. I also didn't want him to take back the money he gave me.

"There, there. Your mother will be here soon. How are you doing in school? Well? If you do better this report card, I will give you a dollar for each grade above ninety percent. Would you like that?"

He caressed my shoulder with his hand as the other remained firmly on my waist. I wore a yellow and pink skirt. My white stockings covered up my panties and was one of the only barriers I had protecting me from Mr. Tanner and his dick juice.

"Mr. Tanner, why are you rocking? There ain't no music." I asked as he moved his waist and humped my bottom.

I felt no sensation but the one growing within my seat. His pants expanded with the size of his dick growing from the pleasure of him massaging my backside. I didn't move, and he maintained his stiffness until I heard a slight grunt.

"Mr. Tanner loves how you make him feel. You make him feel young again. I only rock to good memories. Here's another dollar. When you come home today, I will be here to greet you. Don't tell your momma now, you hear?"

I took the shiny silver dollar, along with the other one he gave me, and held them in my palm. At that moment, I realized that making someone feel good cost money, and they will pay you as long as you make them feel good.

My mother walked out of the house, and Mr. Tanner removed his grip from me allowing me to climb off of his lap. It was too late. My mother already peeped my indiscretion.

"What the hell are you doing on that man's lap? Didn't I tell you not to walk your fast ass over there without my knowing? We are leaving in a few minutes. Wait here."

She rolled her eyes at Mr. Tanner, and he licked her lips at her. Momma ran inside to grab her purse as I looked at Mr. Tanner. He lustfully watched my mother's ass shake beneath her clothing. It took her less than five minutes to get everything she needed. Once again, her eyes met with our elderly neighbor. She didn't bother to say goodbye.

"See you later, Tonya" he said as he rocked in his rocking chair across the hall. He left his door open so he could watch us leave.

"Fuck you, Graham!"

She stuck her middle finger up at him and grabbed my arm, pulling me down the steps. I had no idea where I was going, but I know for a fact that it changed my life forever.

Walk of Shame

"Would you hurry the fuck up? Damn, you walk slow. I knew I should have left your ass at home," she screamed as she pulled me across to the cemetery plot. She was looking for Daddy's grave. She kicked a pebble in the process, and it hit a tombstone in front of us.

Momma began dragging me the moment we walked off of the bus. My Thom McAn black Mary Janes grasped my feet, and my bobby socks cradled my ankles as the stalks of grass tickled the sides. I was tired of walking. We didn't get transfers to another bus so we had to walk all the way to the cemetery. A trip that should have taken us twenty minutes ended up taking us almost forty-five.

"Mommy, my feet hurt. When can we go home?"

I stopped and wanted to sit down, but it wasn't the time or the place.

"Not now, Coryn. I've got some words to say. This will be the last time we come here," she said as we entered Woodlawn Cemetery.

This wasn't the first time we've come here, and I hated it each time. I also usually came with my aunt to bring flowers. It had been a while since me and my mother came together, appearing as the little single parent family we'd been since my daddy died. The last few times I came with my mother, she cried each time. She cussed my daddy's grave too, but this time was worse.

Mommy hated coming here with me because when she cried, I cried, and we had a horrible trip. I didn't want to seem weak in front of her. Today was different. I felt no pain or emotion. She didn't either. My mother walked slowly reading each grave, The liquor made it difficult for her to find it as quick as she usually did.

"Gar-field Tur-ner, here it is... the sonofabitch!"

After walking for what seemed like forever my mother was a disheveled mess. Her dingy brown trench coat was open even though it was cool and crisp outside. Anger fueled the heat within her. My mother stood at the grave that was still fresh with flowers that my aunt and I placed earlier in the week. A wilted yellow rose hung off of the tombstone and petals covered the top of the grave which was still moist from the night's rainfall. I watched as Mommy took out a bottle of liquor out of her purse and began to open it.

She took a swig of it and then began talking loudly. Tears fell from her face as she cussed the ground where he lay. At this point, she let go of my hand and I found a dry place on the grass to squat. I didn't want to be too far from her nor too close. At first, all I heard were mumbles, but her voice grew louder minute-by-minute.

"Mommy, are you crying?" I asked.

She didn't respond. This went on for a few minutes. Soon she began sobbing and began stripping out of her clothing. I stood to the side watching all of this transpire. The trench coat fell to her side. The belt buckle clinked softly as it escaped her fingertips. Her floral wrap dress created the perfect silhouette of her body. Her round derriere poked out and caused the flap to open ever so slightly revealing some of her inner thigh. Even as such a young age, I knew when something wasn't right.

"I can't stand you, you piece of shit. I loved you, and all you did was make my life hell. You fucked around on me to the point where I don't even know what love is anymore. I have nothing to give. Nothing at all! Your own daughter doesn't even know me. She prefers you! I'm nothing to her. I'm glad you are dead! I piss on your grave!"

My mother meant that literally. She cocked her leg to the side and ripped her stockings off. Then she squatted and literally urinated on my father's grave. Air seeped into my mouth as it gaped open. I covered my eyes, but peeked through my fingers. I wanted to stop my mother, but I wasn't old enough for her to listen to me. It made no sense to even try.

As I contemplated if I should stop or distract her, she stumbled and fell on the ground, cussing and slurring her words. It was apparent she had been drinking earlier, which is why she was hostile to our neighbor. He's always rude, but this time she didn't take any mess from him.

"You fuckin bastard. How could you do this to me? I will fix you. You were never shit to begin with. You were born shit, lived as shit, and died as shit!"

My mother tossed the bottle at the tombstone liquor shattered against the flowers that rest below.

"Momma, please stop! Please don't do this. I love you momma!"

I ran over to her trying to change her mind. Alcohol took over her mind, body, and soul. She could no longer comprehend anything that she was doing was wrong. My tiny hand wrapped around her hand as I tried to drag her away. She was too strong and pushed me down. I fell to the ground as dirt and grass stained my clothing. I wiped my face that had been covered in tears.

"Coryn, go sit your ass down. This nigga right here loved you so much that he left you with nothing. That ain't love. Love is giving to someone not because you want something in return, but because you genuinely see the good in them. He didn't love you enough to see the good in me. He wanted pussy. All he cared about was pussy that wasn't even mine. That same pussy that he loved took his life. How's that for LOVE?"

Turning her back to me, she leaned up against the tombstone bearing my father's name, squatted, and shit on his grave. The putrid scent feces coming out of her rear was too much to bear. She almost had diarrhea! I began to throw up immediately.

"Shut the fuck up over there. This is what you will become. SHIT! You are your father's child. A whore. Remember that. He loved you more than me anyway. Whores come from whores!"

Momma wiped her ass with her panties and left them on daddy's grave. I was horrified when she walked towards me, but I had to answer when she called. She was obviously capable of anything. I didn't want to be in her line of fire.

By this time, people that were also visiting their relatives noticed the commotion. The groundskeepers were shocked, and some chuckled at the sight. Others were deeply offended and called the police to report the disturbance. The whole time my mother gave not a damn. Her final wish was to tell my father exactly what was on her mind without regret. She knelt down to me, holding me close.

Tonya Turner was a pretty woman. She wasn't ugly at all. I'm not saying this just because she was my mother. Her hair reached the back of her neck and was wavy. Her nose was broad, and her lips were full. Her chocolate brown skin shone as the streetlights illuminated against it.

Tears fell freely from her eyes clung to her eyelashes. She didn't need any make up. She simply wore lipgloss and that was it. Her breasts heaved up and down as she sobbed into my shoulder. Her hair, peppered with a few gray strands tickled my face. She looked at me, and I knew she was sad.

Her mouth opened to speak and her breath, although reeking of alcohol, was warm. Her hands, although unmanicured, were soft and reminded me of the woman that cared for me. Lately, all she cared about was herself though. I loved my mom, but there was something about my dad that I couldn't shake. And I didn't want to.

"Coryn, now I love you more than your daddy did. I knew today would be our last day together."

"What do you mean our last day?" I said wiping the tears from my eyes.

I was confused because Mr. Tanner said he would see me later. She didn't respond. Instead, she reached into her bra and pulled out an envelope. She pinned the envelope to the underside of my waist along with a note.

"Take this and hide it. Inside is information that will help you when you get older."

She looked around and noticed that police cars had already begun to arrive and circled the graveyard. They watched intently and spoke through their megaphones. My mother ignored them and continued to address me as if it was the last time she would be seeing me.

"Momma, what do you mean? You're leaving me here? Momma, please don't go. I promise I will be good. I will eat all my food and drink my milk like you ask. I will wash dishes even if I have to climb up on the stool. I will get all A's and B's in school, and I will do all my homework. I won't talk to Mr. Tanner. Mommy, please don't go!"

"I love you enough to let you go, Coryn. You will be fine without me, I promise you. I wouldn't do this if I wasn't sure. You will grow up to know what love is on your own terms, and you need to be fine with that. Love is about sacrifice and wanting more for others than you want for yourself."

With those final words, my mother walked slowly towards the street towards a police officer.

"Ma'am put your hands up!"

The police officer drew his weapon and watched my mother carefully for any movements that he deemed threatening. Two more officers appeared and brandished their weapons.

"Fuck you!"

She began walking slowly towards them. The officers cocked back their weapons. I grew frightened and ran towards her. She was all I had left, and I couldn't bear to be without her. I had no choice. As I ran to her, she appeared to run away from me and towards the officers while placing her hand inside of her dress. The officers opened fire! My mother collapsed in a pool of blood at my feet. I arrived too late.

"Mommy! NOOOOO!" I sobbed as I placed her hand in mine and cradled her head in my lap.

Inside of her hand was a picture of us during one of our happier times. I kissed her face. Her breathing was slow and shallow. I watched as life left her body. With every exhale, I watched as a moment of her life left. No more smiles, no more kisses, no more 'I love you.' She was gone. She gave up because one man decided he didn't love her enough.

The sky had grown overcast as it began to drizzle. Her shadow was the sole subject surrounded by nothing but air. It was such a serene sight which suddenly grew gruesome.

I screamed as she took her final breath. After that, my voice remained stuck in my throat for what felt like years. I never recovered from seeing my mother purposely kill herself. I was rendered mute for seven years until I was seventeen, and decided that I had a good reason to open my mouth.

Closed Mouths Don't Get Fed

It was September 1995. I entered the schoolyard of Boys and Girls High School greeted with the scuffles, the screams, and the yells. I already knew what was going down. It was the first week of school, and there was always some drama that carried over from the summer. Whose boyfriend kissed whom, and who he's running after next was always the reason for these fights during the school year.

My silence caused people to do and say things that they otherwise would not. Simply because they thought that I was not smart enough to know what was going on. Many girls and some boys spoke out of turn when they felt they would be safe to do so. I never said anything. Who was I going to tell?

My favorite look was a blank stare which confused people and also caused them to believe I was mute. I was far from mute. I just didn't feel like talking. A lot of good that did. That reason alone caused me to not speak unless it was absolutely necessary. I minded my own business, and did whatever and whomever I wanted. I learned that you could get what you want if you give a little. That's exactly what I did.

"Damn shorty, your mouth is so wet. Yeah, right there. Suck it hard."

He grabbed the back of my head and pushed it down further onto his dick. It was a little smaller than average, but I made it work. The plus was that I could place the entire thing into my mouth to make it appear to be deep-throated. Spit fell out of the sides of my mouth as I hummed on his dick.

"You like that daddy?" I said staring at him in the eyes.

I still held the twenty-dollar bill he graced me with before I began. I had only been doing this for about fifteen minutes and he was already releasing drops of pre cum into my mouth.

I took my tongue and stroked the underside of his dick. I felt him shiver. I placed him back into my mouth and used my right hand to stroke him up and down. The friction from my hand and mouth made it tighter and more like him fucking a pussy. I felt his right hand on my left shoulder as he threw his head back in ecstasy. I went deeper and deeper allowing him to tickle the back of my throat. I gagged and spit on his dick and putting it in my mouth slowly.. Sucking harder and harder, I began to taste his cum.

He throbbed and grew in my mouth. It was time for him to explode and the grunting began within his throat.

"Uhhh, uhhhh, I'm 'bout to cum. Oh shit!"

I held on as he released himself unto my tongue. I kept sucking until I felt him go soft in my mouth. I spit his babies onto the steps, and wiped my mouth with the back of my hand.

"Damn, Coryn. You suck really good dick. You sure you ain't fucking?"

He began to pull up his boxers and his jeans. The belt buckle clanked as it was fastened. It was the only sound, aside from the yelling in the schoolyard, I was able to hear coming from outside.

"I do okay."

I just wanted to go. The plan was for him to just feel my breasts, but he wanted some oral, and he was

24

going to pay me. Why do for free what I can get paid for?

"Nah, you do better than my girlfriend. That's the truth. Anyway, I'm about to dip. You think you can hook me up again later on this week too? Just don't let anyone know."

He zipped up his denim jacket and ran a pick through his hair.

"Whatever you want. You gonna give me something for it?"

I stuffed a piece of gum from my back pocket in my mouth to remove the taste of him from my tongue.

"You know I always hook you up as long as you hook me up."

He looked out of the door to the gymnasium to make sure no one would see him. No one came back there since that's where some of the equipment was

25

stored. The only person that would see was a staff member or a custodian. I heard his footsteps fade away and counted to twenty before I stepped down the hallway. I stuffed the money into my front pocket and was greeted by a deep voice.

"Coryn, why the fuck you just standing there? You missing the biggest fight of the year and it just started!"

My friend, Bumper, grabbed me by the hand and I followed his lead. He had been the only one that understood me ever since I entered that school three years ago. He also had no idea that I liked to suck dick for money. I think it would change his view of me.

He's the only one that I began to trust and the only one that I could voice exactly what I was thinking to. I only responded to him and teachers. Even they believed I was mentally unstable because of how softly I spoke. Often, they had to strain to hear me.

"Bumper, I already know Shaketa and Bree wanted to fight. I heard them beefing in homeroom. Bree is now with Cass, and Shaketa was with him last year. I guess he got tired of being with one person and found someone new during the summer."

I snatched my hand away and checked my Motorola beeper. My best girl friend, Kamerin, hit me up with the code. Every morning she paged me with the code 4-1-1. When that happened, we met in the second floor bathroom to exchange news.

"Bitch, I know you been sucking his dick. I taste your nasty breath when I give him head," Bree said trying to get a rise out of her archenemy.

Her dark hair stayed in a ponytail, but this time she placed it in a bun just in case she needed to do something more drastic to defend her relationship.

27

She threw her bookbag to the side. Her sneakers squeaked against the pavement as she positioned herself. She was ready to fight and assume her position, no matter what it took.

"Well then, we are even because I taste your rotten twat every time I give him head. There should be a law for a woman's pussy to be so stink. You really must do something about that. Maybe instead of talking so much in science, create a douche for your toxic hole."

Shaketa turned around and laughed with those that stood behind her.

By the time she turned around, it was too late. Bree hit her with a right hook causing her to stumble back into the arms of her friends. Shaketa grabbed her jaw which was now split and lacerated. Drops of blood oozed onto her lip. She licked her tongue on it, tasting her wound. She became like a rabid dog, filled with anger inside.

"You fucking bitch. I'm gonna kick your ass. I dare you to touch me again. You ain't bad ho!"

"FIGHT!" were the screams that were heard nearby.

Bree and Shaketa were pushed together and began to scuffle. The girls tumbled and fought back and forth while the crowd surrounded them. Bree grabbed Shaketa's hair and banged her face into the concrete. The group of kids began to chant "Keta, Keta!" Clearly, they wanted her to win the fight.

Popularity always trumped the underdog. No matter what you know, it's who you know that helps you up the ladder of success.

"Wait, stop. They can't fight anymore. Someone's gonna get hurt," Destiny, Bree's best friend said.

She grabbed her friend's hand and tried to stop her from fighting. It was too late though. Bree snatched her hand away and gave her the look of death. Destiny shook her head. Bree always fought and loss. This time she feared it wouldn't end well either.

"Unless you want some too, go sit your ass down. No one is stopping this fight. Cass has to choose and the winner gets to be his girl."

Shaketa's friend Traci stepped to Destiny and was ready to begin their own war. Destiny was never one to be in drama as much as her friend was. She was the voice of reason. Beads of sweat poured off of her face even in the seventy-degree heat, but that was all due to nervousness.

I looked around and noticed Bumper egging on the fight. Past him, Cass was standing against the schoolyard fence watching everything. He loved when women fought over him. It was a power thing. He felt wanted and needed.

Cass was a senior in like me. His midnight skin glistened as if he fell into a chocolate fountain. His teeth resembled Chiclets, and his lips were pink like cotton candy. Rocking Timberlands, Karl Kani jeans, and matching Karl Kani button down shirt, he was the epitome of cool. He was one of those kids that rocked a cell phone and a pager so there was no running to a pay phone for him.

Once his pager went off, he called whoever called him while other unfortunate souls waited for the pay phone to become free. He quickly became the envy of many of his fellow students. Cass was very smart, so smart that he decided to only show up for school when there were exams. Instead of coming to school every day, he used his knack for business to make money. His aspiration was to be a music producer, and he was stacking money to finance his own studio. In the meantime, his hobbies included watching chicks beat this shit out of each other on his behalf.

"Hey, you. C'mere," he called over to me.

I looked right at him, then turned around to watch the girls scratch and claw at each other like cats in heat. That caught him by surprise. He made his way over to the fight. It was like the parting of the red sea. I didn't see it happening, but the way the crowd reacted you would have thought that Moses himself was making his way to us.

No one paid attention to the fact that police were making their way to us also. When they did, they usually placed all offenders in a paddy wagon. No one cared if they were caught slipping. They just needed to be paid attention to by Cass. He was to the senior class what Puff Daddy was to music.

"Ayo, you didn't hear me calling you?" A voice said from behind me.

His booming voice commanded attention. Everyone hushed, trying to decipher where it was coming from. All eyes peered over my head as the voice got closer.

Shaketa and Bree immediately stopped fighting, and their faces were a mess. Bree's hair was strewn all over the place, and Shaketa had a black eye. Still, they straightened up quick and attempted to look cute for the man they fought to impress.

"Didn't you hear me calling you? Are you deaf?"

Cass stepped closer and then stood by my side awaiting a response. The girls looked at me with hate and disgust. I turned around to see Cass staring directly into my face.

"You talking to me?" I pointed at myself in shock because I never thought he would even speak to me, let alone know that I existed.

"Yeah you. I was calling from a while ago. You're Coryn right?" he asked while moving a random piece of hair from my face.

Bumper came and stood next to me and poked me in the rib. He knew I hated talking to strangers. My voice never projected as I wanted it to, and only got worse when I was nervous. Bree and Shaketa looked right at Cass and wondered why he was even talking to me.

"Wait, did he just try to snatch up this ho? After I done got my ass kicked because of him?" Shaketa was the first to speak up, and Bree came to her aid.

"Girl, it was a fair fight. This nigga ain't shit. All he does is use girls. You wanna walk to

34

homeroom with me. I got some shit to tell you 'bout him that no one will believe."

Bree grabbed her bookbag and wiped a spot of blood from her bottom lip. Both girls walked through the crowd and it began to disperse. The police came and shooed everyone away, telling them to report to class. It was the first week of school, and this was the drama that transpired already.

"Come on, let's go to class and leave these fools alone," Bumper suggested. "It's always some drama the beginning of the year. I'm tryna graduate and move. It's too much shit to get into, and I ain't tryna be a statistic. You know a young dude like me is a target anyway you look at it."

Bumper and I walked towards the schoolyard when I realized my laces were undone.

"Go on ahead. I will meet you at our usual spot during third period," I told him as I bent down to retie my shoes.

Suddenly, my shadow disappeared. There was someone standing over me. I was scared to find out, but I knew I would have to eventually see for myself. My crouching position was good for attacking whoever it was and running. I decided to just stand up and see for myself. When I did, I saw him. He looked down at me. The sun reflecting around him made it seem as if he had a halo around his head

"Are you afraid of me?" Cass asked as he stared directly into my eyes.

I stared back at him with no response. His eyes mesmerized me. The way he looked at me caused me to instantly get moist. I was a virgin, but I definitely would have given him some at that moment. The thing is I didn't even know what I would do with him. Besides, I would be just another statistic and a notch on his belt.

"I, I..." I stammered.

My mouth became dry and I wanted to run but where? I had no escape and didn't want to look like an idiot.

"You never speak to me when I talk to you. Today isn't the first time. Are you afraid of me?" he repeated again, speaking more slowly.

His weight shifted from one foot to another, and it was as if the earth stopped moving. All I could see were his pink lips talking to me, but there was no sound coming from it.

"No I am not afraid of you. Ain't like you're God. I just don't like to speak to strangers or anyone for that matter. I stick with what I know," I spat out at him.

He looked taken aback at the response like I rejected him.

"So if you aren't afraid of me, why not speak?"

"You just had two girls fighting over you. Do you think I want to be a part of the harem? No thank you."

I began to walk away. He grabbed my arm causing me to pull back. Cass held up his hands as if protecting himself from harm.

"I'm not going to hurt you. I just want to get to know you. I see how you look at me. I know you want to know me too."

He stroked my face, slowly dragging his finger across my cheek and onto my lips. He was 6'2 compared to my 5'1". I was terrified, but I never let him know.

"I don't care if you think you are going to hurt me. As soon as you feel that you will, you will. It

38

might not be physically, but emotionally. I trust no one, and I definitely don't trust you at all, not with what I've seen. You want me to be your girl? You can't even be my friend."

"Come with me. I don't want you to be my friend."

He grabbed my hand and held it in his. Bumper stood by the entrance to the school and watched the whole exchange.

What he didn't see was how fast my heart was beating. I felt like I was about to keel over dead. I had never spoken to anyone that way before. I truly felt like I expanded my vocabulary and was exhausted.

****

Hours later, my day ended. As much as I was happy, I was kind of sad because the reality of it was my senior year was beginning and it would be my last year. The time had come for me to grow up. After my mom died, I was in and out of foster homes like they had revolving doors. I came, got turned around, and then had to find another.

The last home I was placed in decided to use me to pay their rent. My being there grossed them over ten thousand dollars a year, mostly because my social worker felt that I was disabled. The fact that I didn't speak assisted with that assessment. They diagnosed me with autism, depression, and bi-polar disorder. All of those were incorrect, but I just let them rock. I was tired of trying to defend the fact that I just didn't give a fuck.

That was three years ago. Ever since then I have been my own parent. I didn't emancipate myself, but I plan to when I graduate. No one will be there when I do but at least I can say I did everything on my own.

I learned to forge my foster mother's signature and deposit the checks. Since I had her ATM card, all I had to do is wait for the checks to clear. I was able to sublet studio apartment for a price that was dirt-cheap. Nowadays, all landlords really worry about is that you don't cause damage to their property. They don't even know when I am coming or going.

As I walked down the quiet block of Gates Avenue, I noticed the colors of the leaves were turning red, orange, and yellow. Some of them even crumbled under the weight of my sneaker as I walked over them. What was once green and full of life, was now brittle and cold. Eerily, it reminded me of how my life was with my mother. What was once a woman full of life ended with cold, brittle remains. She was no more and just a mere memory.

I walked into my apartment and was welcomed by Bumper. He was the only one that had a key to my apartment.

"Welcome home. The cable bill is due so it's off, but there's always the radio. We need to be focused on school anyway."

He took my bookbag and greeted me with a can of Pepsi. The aroma of chicken and broccoli tickled my nose.

"Did you order or cook this time? People must think we are married or something since you are always here." I chuckled and kicked off my shoes while sitting cross-legged in the middle of the floor.

"What did you think of that fight earlier today? Dumb chickenheads are always fighting over a dude that doesn't want them."

Bumper focused on a stray piece of thread on his shirt and pulled it to unravel.

"I thought they were stupid."

I didn't want to talk much about the fight because it didn't concern me. I wanted to discuss the man they were fighting over. Cass was a ladies' man that made me feel some way that I couldn't yet explain.

"But what about that dude, Cass? He always got some chicks fighting over him. Remember Jazmine and Erica last year..."

I zoned out at this point. I heard nothing more he said. Instead, the mere mention of Cass' name sent shockwaves down to my nether regions. I began to shift my body to nurse the feelings I was having.

"He ain't nobody. Why are you so pressed to talk about him?"

I got flustered and uncomfortable. I didn't want Bumper to know just how I felt about Cass because I knew how deep his own feelings were for me.

"Yeah ok, Coryn. You like that nigga. You got me here as just a friend, but he sees you and all of a sudden, you forget about me."

Bumper jumped up. Since as I was sitting on him while we were on the floor I was jostled off his lap. His sudden movement had me annoyed, but I know why. I noticed him quietly putting his sneakers on and grabbing his bookbag.

"Bumper, please don't go."

Those were the only words I could muster. He gave me a hug and pushed me against the wall. With my back to the wall, Bumper stared in my eyes. His lips were dangerously close to mine. It felt as if he wanted to extract my feelings from my heart through my mouth. I felt his breath touch my face and looked directly into my eyes. He wanted to say more.

"What I want to say, you will never ever understand. One day you will know what it is to be truly loved. Not for what you have, but for who you are."

Those words pierced my heart like an arrow. I never knew how those words would hold true later on, but I knew that they were going to be important in my life.

****

My mood never recovered after Bumper left. I didn't eat dinner. Instead, I took a shower and went to sleep. When I woke up my apartment smelled horrible from the leftover food .That was the least of my worries.. My mood was even worse and I knew that any and everyone would feel my irritation. and I vowed not to say anything when I arrived at school. As far as the teachers knew, I was sick and wasn't in the best of spirits. I didn't know long that excuse was going to last, but I was not going to speak if I could help it.

I went through my classes normally. Silence can be so loud when your thoughts are yelling at you. Throughout the day, Bumper avoided me when I was trying to get his attention. Later on, I decided to take a walk to the corner for lunch. The lunch truck was out there, and I was tired of eating the same stuff.

With my CD player in my ears, I began listening to Toni Braxton's album. I thought about Bumper. He was so much more than a friend. He was someone I truly loved, just not in the way he wanted me to love him.

I was so into the music I was listening to that I wasn't paying attention and walked into the person in front of me.. Just as I was about to apologize, I realized I bumped smack into the back of Cass, One of the people I wanted to avoid this week. His smirk said it all. He was happy to see me and my grimace spoke the opposite. I wanted to crawl back into myself and not be seen, especially by him.

"Sorry," was what I muttered.

I placed my headphones around my neck and watched him stare at me. His eyes were piercing. His lips, while moving, said nothing that I could hear. They were so pink, like fresh cotton candy.

"I think you did it on purpose because you wanted me to notice you. I've already got my eye on you. You are definitely on my radar."

He dug into his pocket and pulled out a wad of money to pay for his lunch. After tossing a fifty-dollar bill at the vendor, he looked my direction.

Get whatever she wants and keep the change."

His large hands grazed my face and smiled at me. I stood in shock.

"No, No. I will get it myself. Thanks."

I shook my hands and tried to take the money out of the vendor's hand, but it was too late. He already pocketed the change and was ready to take my order. He just had a large ass tip because I wasn't getting anything that Cass had a hand in. As much as I wanted to eat, there was no way I wanted to be associated with him.

"But he already paid for it," the vendor pointed at Cass who stared at me to see if I was going to accept his offer. My thoughts stood firm. I walked away and walked smack into Bumper. He was another person I wanted to avoid.

"Oh, hi Bumper. What's up?" I said with a genuine smile on my face.

I missed my friend. We have never gone a day without speaking. This felt different and out of the ordinary.

"Chillin," he said as he turned his direction to the vendor. "Lemme get a dirty dog, cheese fries, and a Sunkist."

"We gonna chill today after school? I wanted to talk to you about some things."

My eyes were hoping he said yes, and my heart palpitated at his response.

"Nah, I got some shit to handle. Maybe some other time. You seem to be extra busy though, so I'm sure you will be a'ight."

He took his lunch and walked away, but not without giving Cass an evil glare. My heart broke in a million pieces. I loved Bumper but just not how he wanted to be loved.

As I walked home later on that day, I thought about my life and how within a moment's notice life could change. You could love one person one moment and hate them the next. I loved my mother and my father. They loved each other, but it wasn't enough for them to stay around. It made me wonder if my love would ever be enough for others to stay.

Boss Moves

Seven Years Later-2003

I pulled down my Tom Ford shades and observed my surroundings. I hated being in an unfamiliar environment, but it was necessary. The older I got, the more it was required of me to speak. I still had moments where I rendered myself mute in order to avoid situations though. Today wasn't one of those days.

I rarely took unscheduled appointments, but this one was specially requested. One thing I learned not to do was refuse money. That day I refused Cass was one of the moments that changed my life.

It's been seven years since I heard from Cass or Bumper. I've learned to leave my past behind me. As much as I wanted to beg my best friend Bumper to be friends with me again, I had to pull myself up by the bootstraps and keep it moving. Cass only wanted me when I wanted him, and I never gave him the time of day. As much as I wanted to, loyalty was everything to me, and if it caused my best friend to not talk to me then I had to let it go. Later, I realized it was more than Cass. Bumper wanted me and I wasn't ready for that. Oh well.

A woman has to swallow her pride to get things done for herself and her family. Sometimes she has to swallow other things as well!

It may have been only lunch, but what I learned was that particular lunch was the opportunity for me to move forward. I learned that I was denying myself so I had to hustle long and hard to get to what I needed. All money was good money as far as I was concerned. It was a lesson I had to learn, and one that I will never forget.

Driving through the streets of New York City on a Tuesday afternoon, I constantly checked the time. Time was equivalent to money, and money meant happiness in my world. My client said to arrive promptly at two for lunch. I already knew what kind of lunch to expect, but the late factor was none of my concern. I just wanted him to cum on time when I made him and collect payment afterwards. This was something that I learned to do after graduating from high school and took this talent way into college.

"Ms. Barrow, you will arrive at your destination in approximately fifteen minutes. Mr. Elliott has been informed of the delay," the driver informed me.

"Thank you, sir," I said as I continued to look out the window.

Decked out in a black lace dress with tangerine strappy sandals, I crossed my legs in the back of the luxury vehicle. I took a sip of the drink that was sitting in the front compartment as we approached a stop light.

My hands were clammy, yet they held the goblet tightly as I drank the Mimosa that was provided for me. I loved orange juice and needed something to calm my nerves. I was nervous, but confidence took over when I realized it was just another routine appointment. High-powered, sexy and rich... just like I liked them. It wasn't like I had never done this before. It was simply the fact that this person was very prominent in the music industry. If things were to go wrong, it could really go wrong.

Finally, I pulled up to the downtown radio New York radio station. I grabbed my purse and exited the car. The chauffeur opened my door and closed it behind me. That's the thing about having a reputation such as mine. You get treated with the best, and I deserved it.

As I walked inside, I surveyed the office. Many pictures of artists and musicians that I was familiar with caught my eye. I approached the receptionist's desk and spoke without removing my sunglasses. My lips, tinted red by Maybelline, movedin slow motion as I spoke.

"I'm here for Darden Elliott"

"Who may I say is here for him?"

"He's already expecting me," I said to the receptionist as I walked away to have a seat in the reception area.

I had an attitude because I hate giving my name. My clients know when I'm coming. They should let their receptionists and assistants know to just let me in so I could do what I needed to do. I skimmed through a copy of VIBE Magazine to keep myself entertained, hoping I didn't have to announce my presence. I caught a glimpse of the woman rolling her eyes at me. Thankfully, the wait wasn't long. and I was called a few minutes later.

"Ma'am. Mr. Elliott will see you now. He's in suite 1401," the receptionist said a few minutes later.

Perfect timing...a damn good thing because I was about to light into that ass about the stranger's attitude which coincidentally was no better than mine.

"Thank you," I said as I placed the magazine back in its rightful place.

I looked straight ahead to my destination, quickly forgetting the woman behind the desk. She wasn't my focus, and the fact that I was meeting this powerful man caused my pussy to jump. I paid no mind to those who actually had to work for a check. Money that I made in a day, was earned by others in months. months.

After entering the mirrored elevator, I checked my makeup and hair. I adjusted my 40DD breasts and pulled my dress down. My legs looked like chocolate stairways to heaven, and my calves were amazing. A frequent member of the gym, I prided myself on looking fit. Wearing four-inch heels also attributed to my look. I finally arrived at my destination, but before I was able to knock, the door flung open.

"You're late!" said Darden barked at me leaving my hand in the knocking position while he opened the door.

"Yes I am, but you should know this. They told me you were notified," I defended myself, referring to the message that the driver gave me.

I had never met this man before, but I felt comfortable enough to stand my ground. I was worth every penny, and didn't want this bad first impression to dictate how the funds would be distributed. I wanted them right in my pocket like how I enjoyed them.

"It doesn't matter. My time is money. Do you want something to eat or drink?" he said while pouring himself a glass of Absolut vodka.

"No thank you. I enjoyed a drink in the car on the way here," I said while taking a seat on his black loveseat.

I crossed my legs and watched him seductively. Getting comfortable, I removed my glasses, placed them in my purse, and retrieved my compact. I didn't want to give him the benefit of the doubt, but he was so sexy. Being casual relaxed me, and didn't reveal my anxiety.

Darden downed another drink and eyeballed my long, mocha legs. It was a great idea to wear my dress because it complimented my best assets. I sat in such a way that the muscles in my thighs protruded and caused an erection within him.

"Is it hot in here?" I said fanning my face.

My internal thermometer rose to incredible levels watching him move about the room. He was stalking me like I was his prey. The question literally was when he would take me down.

"Nah baby, it's just you," Darden said.

He opened the door and motioned to his assistant, Rose, for her attention.

"Hold all my calls. I will be busy for about an hour or two."

He grinned at me knowingly and Rose responded obediently. No questions asked. He was definitely about his business, and I was right on the to-do list.

Darden closed the office door and the blinds returning his attention to me. Walking over to me, he sat across from me and picked up my left foot. He admired my shoes and smiled.

"I see you received the gift I left for you at the store. It suits you."

"Yes, I appreciated it. A woman loves a great pair of *fuck me* pumps."

He smiled and directed his attention to his erection.

"Well, you will be fucked in those pumps," he said as he removed one foot.

He removed my shoe and carefully placed my foot in his mouth. Darden began to lick between my toes. He kissed them as if he were kissing my lips. It was like he was sucking my clitoris. Careful attention was given to my feet. As I moaned softly, he knew that I was enjoying the feeling.

"Stand up and turn around," he demanded.

He was rather loud, and I prided myself on being discreet. However, I did what I was told and got a glance of New Jersey from the skyscraper windows. We were high enough to see the neighboring state which caused me to daydream. I would love to be away right now, but this was my job. I was more than a high priced ho. I was an escort, a companion, and a lover sometimes. Never however, I was never a girlfriend. I didn't want that title. No good can come from being someone's girlfriend. The situations I've seen proved my thoughts to be correct.

Darden bent me over the couch and pulled up my dress slightly. I didn't wear underwear as he had requested of me. He already had his pants down. His dick was out and grinding up against my swollen slit. He reached over and opened the Mikasa candy bowl on his center table. He pulled out a Trojan condom and ripped it open.

He placed the barrier on his protruding member and entered me from behind. My pussy gushed upon entry, and he pounded me hard and steady. Beads of sweat popped up on the tip of my nose as I felt him grow bigger inside of my tight canal. There was no love making taking place, and my legs remained stiff to maintain my balance. My ass bounced back onto his dick and met his rhythm. He enjoyed it immensely.

"Ohh yeah bitch, fuck this dick. I love a bitch that throws it back. Fuck me baby. Fuck me hard!" Darden said while thrusting deep into me as his balls grazed my clit.

I hated how loud he was getting during sex. I should have expected it since he was he was already loud and demanding during normal conversation. However, during sex everything was maximized.

"Shhh boo, don't make so much noise," I said.

I turned around wanting to change positions and laid my back on the couch. I needed something to shut him up so I began to play with my pussy and placed my fingers in his mouth to suck. Darden took off his slacks and flung them across his center table as he watched me play with my leaky pussy. My pink center was appealing. He grabbed his dick to stroke, preparing to enter the sweet spot once again. If this didn't make him shut the fuck up, I didn't know what would. I traced my lips with my own juices and he licked it off. That was the closest thing to a kiss he would get.

"Why are you teasing me? Give me what I want."

He pulled me close and climbed on top of me, wrapping my legs around his waist.

"You really don't have to be so fucking loud about it. I'm not one of your radio station employees. You might run the airwaves, but you don't run me," I retorted, shaking my head.

He ignored me and lay on top entering me yet again. He placed his hand around my throat. Apparently, I was talking too much, and he wanted to be the one commandeering the situation.

"I'm gonna fuck you 'til it comes out of your pussy and you choke on it," he said while fucking my pussy hard.

He tried to reach over and kiss me, but I turned my face. No kissing was the rule and stipulation. His sloppy tongue caressed my face as sweat dripped off of his forehead and landed on my neck.

"Mmm mmmm mmm, yeah, I like that," I moaned loudly pretending that I liked it.

His volume turned me off or else it would have been good sex. His caramel skin was covered with freckles, and his beard grazed my skin softly. I wanted it to be over and done with. He was much too loud for my liking. I needed it over and done with soon, and decided to put in work for my money.

I gave him my secret weapon and clamped my pussy tightly around Darden's dick in a vice grip. He gasped in pleasure.

"That's what the fuck I'm talkin about. Give it to daddy."

I cringed in disgust. He would never be my daddy. I hated when men said that, but whatever made him feel better. I continued to thrust my hips up towards his. Our hips slapped together, causing friction and allowing him to go deeper into my pussy. He grabbed the top of my dress and released my breasts. He began to suck on them as if he needed nourishment.. He placed one of them in his mouth.

My nipples favored Hershey's chocolate kisses. My arousal level grew to a heightened level. That was my sensitive spot and my pussy radiated an intense amount of heat. I felt an orgasm approaching. Intense twitches of heat and electricity exploded within my waist, and I knew it would come soon.

To achieve that feat, I began playing with my clit. I dipped my finger inside of my pussy and stuck it in his mouth.

After over an hour of fucking, Darden still hadn't had an orgasm, and he was removing more and more clothing to get comfortable. He ended up sitting on the couch and I squatted between his legs and began sucking him off. Up and down, my lips sucked his thick seven-inch cock. Because of his size, I was able to take him all down her throat.

"Oh shit! Yeah, take that dick, you sexy bitch!"

I sucked his dick all the way down to his balls and placed them in my hands to play with. The tip of his dick hit the back of my throat and I gagged due to the thickness. I sucked until spit came out the sides of my mouth and dripped on my breasts. My breasts glistened with my own saliva and his pre-cum. He reached over, massaged it in, and smiled at how nasty I could be.

Slurping, sucking, licking, and face fucking...I was doing everything and he still didn't cum. I wonder if he took a little blue pill.

"Damn baby, suck this dick!" Darden said and began to stroke his dick which was harder than a bag of nickels in a sock. I sucked him off through the condom and felt him throbbing as he approached orgasm. Minutes later I removed my mouth from his throbbing penis, took off the condom and watched him as he stroked it, ejaculating onto my face and neck.

"Ughhhh shit... Fuckkkk Yeah... Ooooooohh," he said as he finally achieved an orgasm.

"Bout fucking time!"

I stood up and pulled my dress up, placing my arms back inside of the sleeves. I retrieved my purse and pulled out some baby wipes. I wiped off his bodily fluids and checked my face in my compact mirror. Most of my make-up was removed due to sweat and body fluid, but I did what I had to do and was getting paid for it. The difference between some of these chicks out here is that I refused to fuck for free.

"Damn baby, you are definitely worth your weight in gold. Is there anything I can do for you to get a repeat performance?" Darden asked while pulling up his pants and buckling his belt.

"You can simply give me what I've earned so I can be on my way. Didn't you mention that you have an event coming up soon? I can accompany you to that as you suggested, but I will not be going home with you at the end of the night. That will cost you extra."

"Baby, you are worth every fuckin' dollar so if I'm paying you are staying!"

Darden handed me an envelope and kissed me on the cheek. He replaced his wedding band that he removed before I entered his office and opened the door to let me out.

"Thanks Dee. We will talk soon about the event," I said as I walked out of the office.

I slipped my shades back on and walked to the elevator. While I contemplated what just happened. A part of me was excited because I had some money in hand. Then again, I was also an accessory to adultery. I looked inside of the envelope. While guilty, I couldn't help but smile.

If a man was content on paying me for what his wife couldn't provide, then who am I to judge? I pressed the button to the elevator and waited for it to get to the floor. A vacation was definitely in order. Where was I to go next? I needed to spend some money to feel better, especially since there was more coming my way.

<u>Confident Not Conceited</u>

After driving through the city and doing some shopping on Fifth Avenue, I arrived at my hotel room and dropped my keys on the table. The benefits of being a mistress is living wherever they wanted you to. I had nothing to worry about. My stay in this hotel lasted for as long as was necessary. I ran right to the bathroom and turned on the shower. I kicked off my high-heeled shoes and placed in them in the accompanying shoebox in their rightful spot in my closet.

My manicured feet sunk into the wall-to-wall carpet as I stood in the middle of the closet exhaling. I'm definitely blessed to be in a situation to have my home paid for. It's good to have rich people in high places. It had been quite a day but nothing I'm not used to. It was time to rid myself of the day, so I grabbed my robe and stepped into the shower to allow the water to beat on my sore body.

The radio in the bathroom was playing soft jazz, setting a mood that caused my body to relax. My pussy was on fire so I massaged it slowly in order to relieve the pressure I was feeling. After I finished my shower, I smelled like fresh squeezed tangerines and oranges from the Victoria's Secret body wash. I grabbed my towel and dried off.

I collapsed on the couch with a glass of wine and decided to check on the messages that I missed while I was with Darden. I pick up my two-way pager. I had over two dozen messages, many of them requesting service well into the end of the year.

Thanks for the great afternoon. I will call you this week for dessert read a message from Darden.

I shook my head and knew that this would be a golden opportunity. Being in the presence of moguls, musicians, and made men would give me the opportunity to grow my network. I knew that there were a few events coming up within the industry, but he never specified.

Nonetheless, I had to be sure that I was on point. I needed to be drop dead gorgeous and that took preparation. It wasn't easy being me, but I made it do what it did. My heart belonged to no one. My mental planning was interrupted by a phone call.

"Hello?" I answered and then took a sip of wine from my goblet.

"Coryn!" said the voice on the other line. It was deep and smooth as chocolate.

"Yes? Who's calling?" I said, placing my glass on the table. The voice intrigued me, yet annoyed me at the same time.

"Coryn?" the voice repeated.

I still wasn't catching it, and I wanted to know if this call was business or pleasure.

"You keep saying my name, but you aren't saying anything. Who is this?"

I grew irritated and got up to pace the floor, opening my balcony door to view the starry sky.

"I'm sorry. This is Gideon. We met at a bar a few weeks ago. I wanted to know if you were interested in going out to get a drink or even dinner?"

"I don't know who you are. Why would I be interested in doing anything like that? All we did was speak casually. I've been to every restaurant in New York City. Nothing interests me anymore."

I rolled my eyes at the truth. I wondered why I even agreed to give him my number and secretly prayed that he didn't call. Now that he did reach out, I had my guard up.

I was with a client the night I met Gideon. Even though I was supposed to be paying attention to my paying customer, I had been eyeing him for a while and my feelings were flip-flopping. He was a friend of my client and he did the polite thing and said hello. At the time, it was already known there was an attraction but we both played it calm and casual. He gave me his number under the premise of business.

"Look, I know it's random, but I am leaving to go to Atlanta in the morning. I wanted to see you before I left. I might have misjudged our communication. And I apologize for that."

Suddenly I felt like a heel for treating him the way I did. It wasn't like he was asking to fuck me. He genuinely wanted to get to know me. I wiped my hands on my robe and placed my hair behind my ears like a giggling schoolgirl.

My hands were getting clammy, and my heart skipped several beats trying to figure out how to accept the invitation. This man was attractive and appeared powerful, but I didn't want to get caught up romantically with someone that didn't understand what my position was as a mistress.

"No wait. I'm sorry. I just didn't want you to think that you could get at me that easy."

I stumbled over my words and tried to figure out how to not let him know he was baiting me and winning.

"I'm surprised you even decided to call me even though I was with someone when we spoke," I continued.

"It's cool. I will be leaving in the morning around eleven. I will have a car come for you at midnight. That should give you enough time to think this over. If you are not in the car, then I know that you are not interested. Good night!" Gideon ended the phone call and the line went dead.

I didn't even have enough time to react. My heart palpitated and I clutched my throat. This man was taking control in a way that I hadn't ever experienced in a potential relationship. He couldn't be serious, could he?

I didn't wonder and tossed on some leggings and a tee shirt just in case. It was just to hang out so I didn't have to get decked out like usual. Funny thing is, I kept staring at my phone, waiting for it to ring.

Frustrated and anxious, I walked into the kitchen to pour myself another glass of wine. With my glass in hand, I went back the couch to watch

BET. That station always had something interesting to watch. This time it was *WOO* with Jada Pinkett. However, I fell asleep not more than thirty minute into it and was awakened by my phone ringing. Startled, I answered it and was surprised by the voice on the other end.

"Come downstairs," the voice said in a deep baritone.

I ran my hand through my hair and placed it in a ponytail quickly to get my wits about me.

"Who is this?"

"You will see when you come downstairs."

The phone call ended. As weirded out as I was, I remembered that it couldn't be anyone but Gideon. The clock on the wall showed that it was half past midnight, and I had been asleep for an hour. I threw on my Reebok high tops and a hoodie, then tossed my phone and mace into a small purse with my keys.

I locked my door, crossed myself, and entered the elevator.

On the way down, I felt butterflies in my stomach. The ride down was one of the longest I had ever experienced. It was filled with nothing but anxiety. I was more intrigued with the fact that he said what he was going to do. I loved a take-charge type of man.

I finally reached the bottom floor and I was greeted by a chauffeur carrying a bouquet of yellow roses, which happened to be my favorite color. I took them and followed him outside. The air was cool, yet comfortable. I was glad I brought my hoodie. The chauffeur held my hand while opening the door to the limousine that was parked outside. I was hesitant, but it was too late to turn back now.

"Hello, Coryn. You made a wise decision in coming to see me before I left. The only thing that would make it better would be if you decided to join me on my trip," Gideon spoke while fiddling with his crimson necktie.

He wore a suit that was tailored to perfection. I could tell he worked out, and his eyes glistened as he stared at me. I was embarrassed that I was so underdressed.

"Hi. I feel so underdressed. I didn't expect you to actually call me. I feel like I should go upstairs and change."

I was met with the resistance of his forearm across my breast. It frightened me, yet turned me on at the same time.

"No don't go. Whatever you need, we will buy. I don't want you to leave. I've gone out of my way to have you here so I would like for you to be able to enjoy every moment." He picked up a bottle of Cristal and poured it into a glass.

"Would you care for some?"

"No thank you. I just want to know what your purpose is for me. I don't usually go with strangers, yet you seem so familiar. I feel like I would have missed out if I declined your invitation."

I glanced out the window and Gideon pulled my face to his.

"If you didn't come, it could have been the biggest mistake of your life."

He tapped on an intercom and directed his driver to pull off. I figured we couldn't be going anywhere too far because he was leaving in a few hours. As much as I wanted to know, I couldn't ask. Trying to figure out my next location was eating at me, but the windows were tinted heavily. I wasn't even able to see a star in the sky.

"We have arrived, sir."

Brandon, the driver, opened Gideon's door. Gideon came around, opened my door, and reached for my hand. As I exited the car, I looked around and realized we were still in the city. I looked up and saw that we were at the Empire State Building. The lights were glowing bright blue and white. I loved seeing the city lit up in such a manner. It was one of the reasons why I decided to stay in Brooklyn.

"Why are we at the Empire State Building? We just went over the Brooklyn Bridge? You made it seem like we were traveling to another state." I questioned his plan for the night, but he gave no further clues.

Gideon grabbed my hand as we entered the building. The Empire State Building closes after a certain time so for him to gain access meant that not only did he have some pull and authority, but he had money too. I didn't know why he was bringing me here, but something inside of me told me that it would be memorable.

"Just come on. You will be fine. You must quit questioning me. Let me show you how I treat ladies that I am interested in."

Gideon guided me into an elevator which took us up the famous New York landmark.

"Oh, so there are more women? I should let them be here instead of me since you have such a choice," I laughed and shook my head.

Gideon walked over to me and cornered me in the elevator. He stroked my cheek and leaned over to kiss my forehead.

"If I wanted another woman, you wouldn't be here. Remember that."

He took my hand and we walked out of the elevator which opened up to the top floor of the building. The city lights illuminated the floor. In front of me was a table decorated with roses and candles. A fine meal was covered with silver domes. Music played softly in the background. It was almost as if he knew to prepare this because his offer sounded too good to refuse. Gideon pulled out my chair, and we sat to eat and drink.

After eating the wonderfully prepared meal of grilled tilapia, baked potatoes, and steamed asparagus, I was ready to find out what Gideon's motives were. I took another sip of champagne and placed a piece of cake in my mouth.

"Why?" I asked him.

"Why what? Why are you here?" Gideon countered.

He already told me to stop asking questions, but I couldn't resist wanting to know why he would go out of his way like this for a women he didn't know.

"Yes. Why? You don't know me and are treating me like either a princess or a whore."

"Well which one are you?"

"Depends on how much money you plan on spending on me. I can be whatever you like."

The liquor was talking to me. As much as I wanted to show my ass, I was waiting on him to show me his first.

"Well, I wanted you to be wined and dined because I believe a gorgeous woman like you deserves the finer things in life."

"I do, but nothing in life is free. You must work hard for it to be given to you, and work harder to pay it off."

I walked over to him. I slowly swung my leg over his thighs and straddled him. My crotch sat on top of his, and I felt his erection rise within my pants. I was turning him on.

"What do I have to do to get you to see that you don't need to pay me anything? I only want your time and love."

Gideon was laying it on thick, but I wasn't falling for it. He wanted sex. In exchange for this treatment, I would give it to him if that's what he wanted.

"You want my time and love or my pussy and some head? Your decision. Nothing is without a fee. You want some ass before you go away. It's cool. You real sexy though, and I want some of you too. It will cost you an extra thousand."

I unhooked my bra and pulled out my breast, slapping my nipple onto his lip. He pulled away and looked at me.

"Coryn, I don't want sex from you. I want to get to know you. All of you. No strings or obligations."

He kissed my neck and lips totally ignoring my breasts. My nipples were so erect when I placed them back inside of my shirt, the imprint was very prevalent. I wanted to know why we weren't fucking.

"Are you married or gay? Which one is it?" I countered.

"Neither. I am single and straight. I am not even mad that you accuse me of that. You will come around soon enough. When you do, I will be right here waiting for you."

Gideon picked me up and placed me on the ground. His arms were so strong that I briefly felt secure within them. He reminded me of Bumper. Maybe it was the liquor, but I wanted to make love to him I placed my hand on his crotch and began massaging it slowly. I felt his nature rise. heavy breathing escaped from his lips. Gideon looked at me like he didn't know whether he should stop me or continue to succumb to my plans of seduction. My answer came with his actions.

He picked me up and shifted his weight. I sat down and stared at him. still trying to process what just happened. With my breasts out and me caressing his body to the point of arousal, he still rejected me. I wasn't pleased.

"When are you leaving?" I changed the subject.

I was ready to go home. I felt rejected and needed to call someone to fuck and go to sleep.

"As soon as Brandon drives us to your home, I'm going right to the airport. I've got a private jet to take me to Atlanta. From there, I have business in the Bahamas. I will return in a week. That should give you enough time to figure out if you want to see me again."

I nodded and turned my back to him. The sun was now rising. We watched as it lit up the skyline. People down below were just waking up, and it was time for me to go to sleep. Gideon held me tight as we watched the sun shine on our faces. His hand around my waist felt so secure. I couldn't get caught up in him and this feeling. Besides, it was the liquor speaking. I wanted to be doing so much more with him. I liked his style. Hours of talking and getting to know him made our connection real, like we knew each other before. Funny enough, he never spoke about his childhood. Since I endured so much drama as a child, I was also very vague about mine also.

It was time to go home. I rode silently in the car. He woke me up minutes later. I had no idea how tired I was. When I arrived, he came out of the car and walked me to my brownstone.

"It was very good seeing you. You should get some rest. I need your energy when I return in a week. Whatever you need, just call me and I will deliver even if I am away. Until we meet again, my dear."

Gideon kissed me on the forehead and on my cheeks. His scent invaded my nostrils. causing me to be lightheaded. This man definitely turned me on. I had to get him out of my system. but it was too late. He clouded my thoughts and judgment because I actually cared about what he thought. While he was gone, I would have to resume business as usual. No man is deserving of my heart yet.

Money, Power, Respect

It was already early morning when I arrived home. I took a hot shower and climbed into bed. My dreams were filled with the last few hours and how wonderful Gideon made me feel. I didn't need clothes. I more than likely was going to play with my pussy as soon as I woke up.

It was about noon when I received a call on my phone. I couldn't even find it since I left it in the living room. I damn near broke my neck trying to locate it. My breasts bounced as I ran through the house from my bedroom to the living room to retrieve the call before it ended. I was breathless.

"H-hello" I said hoping to not sound too rattled. It wasn't who I wanted. I was pissed.

"Well hello. I've been texting you all night and morning. Did you forget our gym session in midtown?"

It was my best friend Alayna. I met with her every morning at seven o'clock to workout. Since I'd been out with Gideon all night, I missed our workout.

"Hey girl! Dammit. I totally forgot. I overslept. I had a hard day at work."

Hysterical laughter broke out on the other end of the phone. This bitch was clowning me! Alayna sounded like she was choking on the other end of the phone. I heard her gasp for oxygen.

"Bitch, I know you aren't laughing so damn hard. I work just like you." I said sticking out my bottom lip in a pout. "Bitch, you're just jealous because I make more money than you and I like what I do. I earn in a day what you make in two weeks!"

"You think I want to spread my pussy apart for multiple men? I've got my husband. It's not that serious to me. I can crochet for all that."

Alayna was getting annoyed with the way the conversation was going.

Alayna was a thirty-something married woman with no kids. She wanted to live her life the way she saw fit, but her husband was very controlling.

She grew up in Queens, New York to a single teenage mother. She and her mother were so close that they literally were each other's crutch. Alayna's mother got herself together and she and her daughter graduated with honors from Webster Community College in Biology and Psychology respectively. Alayna went on to pursue her doctorate and became a pediatric nurse. She always wanted more for me than she wanted for herself and always seemed annoyed when jealousy was mentioned.

"Well crochet me a scarf so I can tie one of them son of a bitches up. We can go shopping for shoes after."

I couldn't help but laugh. I cared less what people thought about me and my business. I had moves to make, and wasn't letting anyone stop my flow or my money. I refused to struggle or beg from anyone. My money was my own. When a man has control of that, you are screwed. I was at no one's beck and call, but my own.

"I wear an eight, so just say the word. Anyway, Seth wanted to know if you were still going to Aruba in a few months for our couple's getaway and who are you taking?"

I thought for a second and realized that I had no steady partner, nor did I have any idea who could accompany me. I would take Darden, but I didn't want him to get too comfortable with my company. He's the type of man that could get addicted. Besides, what would he tell his wife?

This was pleasure, not business. He wouldn't pay for everything.. I shook my head and sighed heavily, exasperated at this simple question that caused me to take a hard, close look at my life and my history with love and relationships.

"No clue, but I will keep you posted for sure as the date approaches. If all goes well, y'all will have to pay little or nothing. That will be my gift to you."

I actually thought about inviting Gideon, knowing that it was something he would be interested in doing and I wouldn't have to pay a dime.

Alayna sucked her teeth and cleared her throat. She didn't want any of my sugar daddies paying for something that was for her and her husband to enjoy. She was capable enough to finance her own vacation. Inviting me as her best friend was an added bonus.

"Yeah, ok whatever you say. I gotta go check on some things for Seth. Maybe you should consider slowing down and falling in love. Whatever you're looking for can't be found at the tip of a dick. We will talk later."

"Love? Who the fuck wants to fall in love? It ruins everything. Later," I said, hanging up the phone.

I hated fighting with her, but she had to live her life despite what anyone thought. Alayna didn't complain in the past when she was able to come on trips with me. Marriage had turned her into a judgmental bitch. Apparently, she felt better than everyone else.

I threw the covers over my head to sleep some more. I ignored my Blackberry that kept going off. I know some of the messages were business and some of them were Gideon, but he could sweat it out a little and miss me. The others could wait. They always came back, and I was content in just relaxing.

****

Four hours later, I woke up not realizing how tired I was. My phone kept ringing off the hook and my pager battery died. I guess whoever was paging and texting me finally stopped. I stretched and got my wits about me. Still drowsy, I stumbled to the bathroom and washed my face. I grabbed my robe from behind the door and threw it over me. I was tired, but no longer sleepy. I was definitely sexually frustrated. Gideon definitely put a move on my body and heart. I hated how I thought of him constantly. He ruled my mind and soul already. I wasn't going to get caught up. I couldn't or else no good would come of it. Love wasn't made for me.

After seeing what happened to the only man I've ever loved, my daddy, I wasn't too sure that I wanted to go down that road. After taking a shower, I grabbed some clothes and sat on my sofa to finally get back in the groove of things. The night was young, and I still had a few appointments to handle. I logged into my AOL account to see that it was full of appointments. I had several lined up for the next two weeks and some that went into the new year. I was determined to make this year better than last year.

My first of two appointments of the night were in an hour and I needed to haul ass. I walked into my closet and grabbed the easiest thing that I could - a little black dress. I pulled out my black pumps and slipped the dress over my black lace bra and thong. I applied my makeup and was ready within minutes. By the time I was ready to go downstairs, my phone rang signaling that my driver had arrived.

I walked down and saw a woman holding a red rose. It was a first for me. I expected to see a man, but, hey, whatever works..

"Hi Coryn! So nice to finally meet you."

The woman gave me a kiss on the cheek, looked me in the eye, and then planted another kiss on the other cheek. I was taken aback, but I went with the flow.

"Hi. Nice to meet you tooShe knew my name before I knew hers.

"Oh, excuse me. I'm so sorry. It's Shai. My name is Shai Cardona."

She grabbed my hand and we walked out of my building. Parked at the curb was a black Escalade. The driver opened the door for us. Inside was a gentleman that I had never seen before, but I was sure he was the one that I had been corresponding with.

"Kaine, isn't she lovely? She looks just like the photo we saw," Shai, said smiling. She climbed into the car and sat next to the man.

"Coryn, this is my husband. He's been corresponding with you on my behalf. We want you to have a threesome with us."

My eyes bulged at the request. I was under the impression that it was just me and him, but to add another party into the mix caused shock. Then a moment of clarity set it. Since it was two of them, I could get paid for satisfying two bodies. The dollar signs calculated in my head.

"Well this is a first. I hadn't anticipated something like this. You do know that, as a mistress, I am being paid to satisfy one person. The price changes when there are additional parties." I tried to sound as professional as possible without making it seem just about the money.

Kaine looked at Shai and they kissed each other passionately. I was getting a bit turned on already and I hadn't even begun anything. I had another appointment later on that night, but this one would surely be interesting.

"Yes, we are very aware. You see my wife is bisexual and she's unsure of how to pleasure a woman. I know how to eat pussy, and I eat hers well. I need for you to pleasure her so she can feel what I experience. We don't even have to have sex," Kaine said placing his long, light brown dreadlocks into a tight ponytail. His light brown skin shone under the New York City lights.

"Are you down? I find you very sexy Coryn." Shai reached over and touched my leg. I smiled and nodded.

"Great, so let's make this happen shall we. I booked us a room at the Times Square Marriott. It's a neutral spot since we live uptown, and only the best for my wife and the woman that will be popping her cherry," Kaine told us and I smiled nervously.

Clearly, they expected a lot from me, so I would have to deliver my A-game.

We entered the Marriott lobby and everyone watched us enter as Kaine held the small of my back. I gripped Shai's hand and we made our way to the front desk. The room was already booked so the attendant checked us in and handed us our room key which coincidentally 690.

How fitting, I thought.

"Are you ready?" Kaine asked once we entered the room.

He walked over to the curtains and opened them wide enough to see over the city below. Many buildings and lights shone in a variety of colors with billboards. Flashing lights danced on the sheets of the bed while everyone settled and figured out how this was going to begin. I had never had a ménage a trois before and had no clue where to begin.

"I must admit, this is a strange request."

Shai sat next to me and began slowly playing with my fingers. For someone who had no idea what she was doing, she certainly knew how to turn me on. Kaine tossed his slacks and button down shirt on a chaise lounge that sat in the corner of the room. He walked over and knelt down between my legs. He picked up Shai's leg removing her shoe. He slowly kissed her toe, sucking it gently in his mouth and made his way up her ankle to her thigh.

Aroused, she lay back and allowed him to have his way. She still had on her skirt and he placed his hand beneath it causing her to jerk up. He hit a spot. I leaned over and opened a tiny button on her blouse and her breasts spilled out of it. Kaine looked up at me in approval and I finished removing the clothing that stood in the way of our venture.

"Wait, let me."

She sat up and removed her blouse, tossing it to the side and revealing her sapphire blue Victoria Secret bra. That soon came off, and her breasts were a light caramel color. Her areolas were darker than her complexion but still sexy. Her nipples were tiny and bite sized. As if he read my mind, Kaine placed his lips on one of her breasts and sucked. "Mmmmmm damn baby, you feel so good."

Shai threw her head back and I removed my dress, leaving it on the floor. I sat down on the bed and began to take off my heels but Kaine's hand stopped me.

"Leave them on," he commanded and I lay back on the bed.

I kept my bra on as I felt a pair of hands exploring my thighs and pushing them to opposite sides. Soon I felt lips kiss my pussy lips and a tongue delve itself into my sweet spot. I gasped and my hands moved towards my captor. I felt a handful of soft shoulder length hair and I pulled back. At that moment, Kaine's hands gripped my wrists and I felt his dick on my lips. I did what came naturally and began sucking it while his wife tongue fucked my pussy. I moaned softly and he leaned over placing his finger inside of her ass hole. I continued to wet his member and sucked harder as she nibbled on my clit.

"Damn ma, you are really feeling this," he said watching his wife invade my private area.

I gushed in her mouth as she hit a spot that brought me to orgasm. Kaine moved off of the bed and positioned himself behind her.

Entering her pussy as she sucked on my clit, he caused her to moan loudly. My hands grabbed the sheets and I felt her teeth graze my clit with each thrust. He pulled her head back and I was able to see my juices glistening on her lips. I sat up and kissed her, tasting myself on her lips. Kaine watched that and began to thrust harder.

"Come and lay down so you can lick her slit," he demanded.

I did what I was told and lay so that her pussy was positioned over my tongue. His dick was still inside of Shai and grazed my lips. I tongued his balls while it traveled the distance of her pussy. I licked the drops off of him that leaked unto my mouth. Raising my head up, I found her clit and stimulated it with tiny licks and kisses.

"Oh my God. Baby, I'm gonna cum. Baby, hold me please."

Shai shivered and trembled as a powerful orgasm invaded her body. Kaine held her close as he released his own orgasm within her body. I, still underneath them both, tasted their juices until they were finished. They lay on the bed on top of one another and I sat up.

"Wow, you were phenomenal. You sure you never did that before?" Shai asked in a whisper as she recovered from her climax.

"I had never done anything like that before. I guess I just did what came naturally." I said grabbing a sheet from the bed and wrapping it around myself.

I headed to the bathroom to wash up and gargle. I had business to tend to and this was only one of my appointments for the night. I returned and picked up my dress off of the floor to get myself together. Kaine and Shai were cuddled up in the bed, grinning at each other.

"Thank you so much. I think we will be doing this more often. If you want, we would love to have you with us again. You really brought it out of us."

Kaine picked up his boxers off of the floor, and I watched his dick swing from side to side. Even after what we did, I felt embarrassed and turned my face from him.

"No problem. Now if I can be so frank, I would like to be paid. I know it was brief, but there was no penetration on my end. Nonetheless you were both satisfied by me."

I reached into my purse and pulled out some lipstick and my compact. I applied it and fixed my hair which was disheveled.

"Oh no, not frank at all. Business is business. We will write you a check for seven thousand dollars. Is that sufficient?"

Shai grabbed her purse off of the nightstand and a pen. She handed it to Kaine who wrote out a check for seven grand and handed it to me along with their business card. He was a mogul in his own right as a clothing designer and she was an entertainment attorney.

"Thank you. I appreciate everything and good luck."

I tucked the card into my clutch and walked towards the elevator. I needed to get back to my apartment and prepare for my next client. Luckily, they didn't get rid of the driver that brought me to the Marriott.

"Ma'am, are you ready to go back home?" He opened the Escalade door and I entered. "Feel free to have anything back there to eat. I know you have been running all day."

As soon as he said that I noticed there were finger sandwiches and drinks waiting for me. These people were prepared to cater to my whim. I wonder how much they would pay me to be in a polyamourous relationship with them .

Who am I kidding? I've got way more people to please aside from them. I had some finger sandwiches and drank something just in time to pull up to my building.

"Thank you."

I exited the vehicle and went upstairs to clean up a bit before my next client. My phone rang as soon as I stepped out of the shower and started to get dressed again. I tossed my items back into my bag and reapplied my lipstick.

"Ms. Turner, your car has arrived," the doorman notified me.

As I walked downstairs, he greeted me and walked me out to a black Lincoln Town Car. My date was inside for the night.

Presidential Sweets

"Hello Jameson," I said, greeting him with a kiss on the cheek.

I hoped that I would be able to satisfy him for the night. I was getting tired, but the money for this one would far surpass anything I did earlier in the evening.

"Looking gorgeous as always," he replied as he watched me pull out my compact to check my makeup. "Are you ready for the evening? It's a political function and I needed a lovely lady on my arm. I know many have used your services, but the story is that you are a friend of my daughter that graduated from Yale law school and is interested in throwing her hat in the arena as an intern. How does that sound?"

I didn't care what it was so long as he gave me my money. That thought alone reminded me that I needed to get paid before anything transpired.

"I'm ready. Before we go any further, may I have the deposit, please? I'll take the remainder at the end of the evening."

He reached into his lapel and pulled out a check in the amount of three thousand dollars. Jameson Reynolds placed it in the palm of my hand, but not before kissing me slowly and deliberately on the shoulder leaving a love bite. At fifty-five years old, he was still sexy.

His tuxedo fit him perfectly and he smelled like Versace Metal Jeans. It was sexy and intriguing. I was actually turned on. I never had an issue with catering to older men. I had been doing it all my life.

He slowly slipped his hand between my legs and I let him feel how wet I was.

"Careful or we won't make it to the banquet," I said as I gripped his wrist. He flicked his finger around my thong and shifted it to the side, dipping his middle finger inside of me. I shivered in the seat. I was getting turned on and placed my hand on his crotch. His erection grew in his pants and I was impressed. He definitely didn't seem like the type to need Viagra.

"I don't care if we get there or not. All I want to do is cum with you," Jameson whispered into my ear. I blushed as he spoke dirty to me.

He made it clear that we would be having sex. Quite honestly, it didn't bother me one bit as long as he was paying me. We arrived at the Metropolitan Museum of Art and were surrounded by councilmen, senators, and many influential New York City politicians.

I had fucked many of them. It didn't bother me because they had their wives with them. Just like I didn't want to be revealed, they had secrets to keep. If the situation arose, I'd just pretend I was meeting them for the first time. It was safer that way.

"We are here, sir," the limo driver said. He stopped the car and opened the door for us.

I was used to this treatment from my clients. It was one of the perks of the job.

"Thank you, Travis. Please be here to get us at 1:00am. We'll be going to the Hotel Pennsylvania afterwards."

Travis replied and Jameson took my hand for us to enter the event. He was always the gentleman and never treated me like a whore. I was only one when he paid me at the end of the night.

"Are you ready?" he asked me.

I smiled and nodded. I was ready to eat some good food and get some new contacts. A lot of my dates were obtained by mingling with my current dates. This was a definite benefit because these men had money, and that's one thing that I loved almost as much as sex.

"I'm all ready to go. This should be an interesting night. I can't wait to meet all of your friends and learn all about the business." I smiled up at him as we walked in and settled by the door.

I truly was interested in learning more about him and politics. So many things happen behind the scenes that we aren't privy to. This was my way of finding out insider secrets without feeling guilty.

During the course of the evening, I did just that. I heard about election rigging, ponzy schemes, and the like. I was intrigued, and turned me on to know so

117

much more about the underhanded things and bureaucracy that took place. These men fought like cats and dogs to win, yet all the information was received at events like this. Smart, if you ask me. I excused myself to use the bathroom. I was a stall in the ladies room when I heard angry voices.

"She's fucking him. I can tell. I can't believe he brought that bitch here knowing that I would be here."

"Janet, how do you know that they have something going on? It could be nothing."

I sat on the toilet and remained quiet while I peeked through a small crack in the door. I prayed silently that they weren't smart enough to check to see if anyone was in the stalls. They appeared more concerned with who was having relations with whom.

"I know he is, Tanya. The way he looks at her. The way she touches him, and the gentle placement of his arm around her waist. I can tell because he used to do that shit to me. Congressman Jameson Reynolds is fucking his intern. I used to be his intern so I know all of his tricks."

"Well, which one are you referring to? There were several of them in there." Tanya said trying to diffuse the situation. I waited patiently to see if they would mention and or describe me.

"Janet, she's got on a black dress. She's the one that came with Jameson. Trust me, I know how he is. He's acting the same way with her that he used to with me."

She grabbed the soap and began washing her hands vigorously. "I know how one acts when they are fucking their boss. I used to fuck him well." She rinsed and took up a hand towel to dry.

Now that I knew that they were talking about me, I decided to make my appearance. It wasn't my fault that Congressman Jameson chose to be with me tonight. Besides, I can't get paid if I'm hiding from jealous women in the bathroom. The bathroom door clicked and I walked out with my clutch under my arm. I greeted the ladies with a nod.

"Ladies! Such a lovely event, isn't it?"

I began washing my hands and dried them on the hand towels that the attendant gave me. I reached into my purse and tipped her twenty dollars. Not my money so I had no problem sharing. They spit daggers at me with their eyes as I felt them watching me walk away.

I sashayed out to find Jameson mingling and walked right over and whispered in his ear. I was ready to go, and needed some sex to help me feel a little better about myself. It's not like I felt guilty. I was simply horny. If I was going to be accused of sleeping with him, I might as well do it.

"Excuse me gentleman. Ms. Turner seems to be under the weather, so we're going to call it a night. I will speak with most of you all in the week. Be well."

He placed his hand around my waist as I said goodbye.

"Good night. It was a pleasure talking to each and everyone of you."

I saw the ladies from the bathroom, Janet and Tanya, and I smiled at them also. I wanted them to know that they were correct about me but there was nothing they could do.

As Jameson and I walked to the car, I thought about how easy this life was. I thought about my mother and how stupid she was to fall in love. Love brought you nothing, but pain and regrets. The only thing I ever loved was money, and that shit never left my side. Life was getting better and better each day and as I sat in an expensive car with a high profile date I realized that I didn't choose this life. It chose me.

We made our way to the Hotel Pennsylvania and up to our room. It was already prepared for our night together. The room was lit with candles and the king size bed was made perfectly. I loved how Jameson made me feel comfortable with even the small things that he provided me with. When I was with him, I never felt like the woman I was. He and I had been dealing for over three years, and I was always his main priority when I was with him. No wonder the women at the charity ball seemed jealous of me.

On the bed was Victoria's Secret lingerie that he left for me. It was baby pink with a g-string to match. The bust was decorated with rhinestones. I grabbed a towel and took off my dress, hanging it in the closet nearby. I left my shoes on because I knew Jameson would want me to wear them. After my shower, I came out and began to lotion my body.

Jameson had remained down at the hotel bar to give me some time to get ready. He usually takes that time to wind down and do a little networking. By the time I placed my other shoe on and lay across the bed, I heard the key card unlocking the door to our suite. He was kind enough to bring a bottle of wine from the bar.

"All ready for me?" he asked as he slung his suit jacket across the back of the chaise lounge. He kicked off his shoes and sat on the edge of the bed. I crawled up behind him, placing my breasts on his neck. He felt my warmth radiate against his skin.

I kissed his face slowly and beads of sweat appeared. My hands caressed his neck and I removed his tie. I opened my legs so his back leaned against my taut stomach. I placed my right leg in his lap and grazed his erection. His large hands cradled my feet and played with my toes.

Jameson had an amazing foot fetish, and always made sure to give me money to get weekly pedicures. I never knew when one or all of my toes would end up in his mouth. His wife had all ten toes, but had an extra toe on one foot and only four on the other. He loved her, but her feet were definite turn off. I wonder if she knew that was one of the reasons why they hadn't had sex in three years.

"I'm as ready as I will ever be for you. Whatever you need me to do, I will."

Jameson got up and removed his slacks, briefs, and socks. I was lying on my back and waiting for him. Jameson climbed between my legs and removed my panties. He sniffed them before tossing them aside. He loved how I smelled. I kept my pussy shaved and smelling good just for him, even going as far as to have it vajazzled at times.

His chiseled body did everything for me. Tender butterfly kisses landed on my thighs. I moaned slightly, becoming instantly turned on. His lips made their way to my sweet spot, and my hands instinctively reached for his head. His salt and pepper curls twisted around my fingers. I massaged his scalp and gripped his head, directing him to apply pressure. My clit grew engorged as I gushed onto his tongue with every lick.

"Ooooh yeah baby. Get that," I moaned as I threw my head back in pleasure.

I pulled him up and had him lay on his back while I positioned myself on his face. My sweet flavor remained on his lips even after he removed it. His tongue glazed with my nectar yet he continued to ingest every drop of me. While he worked on me, I buried my face in his thighs and his pink dick deep into my mouth. My intention was to swallow him whole, but not before he and I did some damage.

"Ooh Coryn, you know how to make daddy feel good."

I cringed when I heard the word daddy, but I had grown accustomed to it. I simply sucked harder. His cock grew in my mouth tickling my uvula. I took it out my mouth and spit on it. Drips of saliva mixed with pre-cum escaped from the sides of my lips. I placed him back in my mouth and sucked harder than a Hoover vacuum. My tongue flicked the tip and I felt him shiver and shake.

At that moment, he bit my clit gently. The pressure was enough for me to cum hard and gush rapidly unto his tongue. I felt him growing in my mouth and climbed off of him. I grabbed a condom off the nightstand and placed it on him. His pink cock grew harder within my grip.

"Are you ready for me baby?" I said laying him down to straddle him. Jameson seemed breathless, but I figured it was because he was so aroused. His normally pinkish white skin was almost ashy-grey. He was pale and his breathing was shallow and labored. I was concerned, but not so much that I wanted to stop. He started it and I was going to finish it.

"Yes, give daddy what he needs to survive."

That sounded kind of off to me, but I paid no mind and mounted him. The walls of my pussy gently caressed his shaft. I felt myself contract immediately and I gasped at the feeling. Jameson's pink dick pounded my chocolate canal and I gripped the back of his head for leverage.

Up and down, I bounced and rode him as his hands gripped my ass cheeks. His hands felt clammy, but I just attributed it to sweat and being very aroused. My wetness soaked his lap as I gained momentum and our rhythms matched each other. I kissed his lips and face as my breasts tickled his chin. Beads of sweat developed on his face and I wiped it off.

"Thank you baby, Thank you! Oh shit. You sure know how to make daddy feel good."

His glazed eyes stared at me and something felt off. I didn't know what it was, but I certainly felt like he wouldn't be okay. I had been with him long enough to know when he didn't look and feel like himself. It wasn't just an increase of stimulation.

Despite the warnings, I continued to fuck him and felt his pace quicken. Caught up in the moment, I failed to recognize how labored his breath grew.

Within minutes, he picked me up and threw me on the bed to climb on top. He didn't miss a beat and brought my left leg up in the air. All of sudden his energy was between my thighs and I felt like my pussy was about to explode.

"Oh yeah baby. Yes, give it to me. Give me that fat white cock. Fuck me like you own this pussy!"

It felt too good and I had to remember who it was. He never had sex with me like that before.

"Uhh yes. Yes baby I'm coming. Daddy is coming home," Jameson yelled out in ecstasy.

His face turned beet red with a large vein sticking out of his neck. He was sweating so profusely that some of it dripped into my eyes.

Suddenly, Jameson screamed as he achieved orgasm. A guttural scream came from the pit of his stomach. I watched as his eyes rolled in the back of his head and he collapsed onto my breast, spent and tired. I wiped my face and stared at the ceiling. My stomach rumbled. Something was wrong. I had neglected to listen to my heart and my sixth sense.

"Whew baby, that was amazing."

I rubbed his hair and kissed his cheek. There was no response so I ran my fingers through his salt and pepper hair. There was still no response.

The Still of the Night

"Jameson, sweetie, did I wear you out?"

I moved him off of me and collapsed back onto my chest. My hand landed on his neck and I felt nothing. I placed my face near his lips and felt no breathing. . His dead weight remained behind me. I grabbed a sheet from the bed and wrapped it around me. What was I going to do?

I sat on the floor with his hand in mine, hoping and praying he would wake up. No such luck. Every time I heard room service, I jumped. The silence was deafening. My heartbeat sounded like banging within the confines of the silent room. Finally, I placed the "Do Not Disturb" sign on the door. That would last until checkout.

Shit! How could I check out without him since the front desk clerk saw us entering the hotel together? If he didn't come out, people will wonder what happened to him. They will think I killed him.

For some reason my thoughts drifted to my best friend Bumper. I missed him. He would know what to do. If only I kept him close. I always knew how to fuck things up. Death was something I was relatively used to. People always left me in some shape or form.

What was I to do? Who was I to call? Who could help me? Just then, I heard a soft hum. It was my pager. Crawling across the room, I retrieved my pager from my purse. Three messages from Gideon were displayed. He missed me. He couldn't wait to see me. Do I miss him? So many questions and I had the answers to none. I did however have a simple question for him - Could he help me?

I paged him and gave him the number off the front of the hotel phone in the room. It rang back, immediately causing my heart to jump. The clock ticking and my heart beating were the only sounds in the room. Jameson wasn't breathing, and my brain was on overdrive trying to figure out what to do.

"Hello?" I spoke barely above a whisper as if not to awaken the already dead body.

He remained right where I left him, and his body temperature was already beginning to drop. It had been almost two hours.

"Coryn, what's up? Where are you?" Gideon sounded so sexy.

His deep baritone voice echoed into the phone and tickled my eardrums. After the night I had, I needed a semi-familiar tone.

"I'm at the Hotel Pennsylvania and in room 1436. Something terrible has happened. I didn't want you to find out this way."

Tears welled up in my eyes and I wiped them away He was the first person that I really connected to in years. I didn't understand why he was the one person that I decided to call, but I just needed someone to talk to and save me.

"I'll be there in fifteen minutes." Without questioning, he responded and I felt just a little bit safer already.

I must have held the phone for a long time because when someone knocked on the door, I was still holding the phone in my hand. I quickly hung up the phone and ran to the door. I looked through the peephole to see who it was. Scared and anxious, I saw Gideon standing there in an olive green trench coat. A man I didn't know stood beside him. I let him in and wrapped the sheet further around my breasts.

"Are you okay? This is my best friend, Terrance. I don't know what happened, but you sounded like you needed more than just my help."

He smiled and pulled me close. I shivered in his arms due to nerves. Nervous sweat poured my nose and he wiped it off., .

"I'm okay. There's something I need to tell you. It's been bothering ever since you left. I wanted to tell you, but I didn't know how."

I felt he needed to know my secret before he got knee deep in my bullshit.

"No need. Terrance is a captain in the police department and a very good friend of mine. Nothing you don't want revealed will be."

Gideon stepped aside as Terrance stepped forward and shook my hand. My wrist, with my lack of energy, dangled in his firm grip.

They walked into the room and surveyed the area. As I watched Jameson's lifeless I sighed not knowing how I got myself into this predicament. If I knew this was one of the risks of this job I would have never began.

"I am a mistress. I have sex with men for money and companionship. They are in positions of power, and I enjoy the finer things in life. It's a fair exchange," I blurted out, unable to contain myself.

I walked over to the window and almost tripped on the sheet I used to cover myself. Terrance grabbed a robe that was in the closet and placed it around my shoulders. I draped it around myself and secured the sash around my waist. I felt so ashamed, and Gideon saw how uncomfortable I was.

"Coryn, I know who you are and what you do. It's never stopped me from loving you before. You can call me Bumper from now on, if it makes you feel comfortable."

He smiled and caught a view of my glares which caused his grin to melt away instantly. My heart beat rapidly like an African drum and skipped several beats. I couldn't believe that my best friend was standing in front of me all this time and I had no idea.

I had a million questions and spit them at him at rapid-fire speed.

"What? How? Where have you been? Did you know all this time? Why didn't you say something? How could I not have known?"

"What the fuck do you mean to call you Bumper? Do you know who that is?"

Gideon reached out to me and I swatted his hand away. A rush of anger grew within me as I began to see red. I didn't want to hear his lies.

"Let me explain, Coryn. I promise I'm Bumper. I'm your best friend from the Stuy. Remember we went to Boys and Girls?"

My head got dizzy and light. This was way too much to handle. His friend, Terrance, brought me back to reality.

"This reunion will have to wait until we have disposed of the body. I will call in my squad and let them know how we are gonna handle this. Take her and everything else she owns out of the hotel. The car is waiting out back. Don't worry, son. She's definitely worth the trouble."

He tossed Bumper the keys and a bag.

I was given some sweats and sneakers to wear just in case my clothing contained evidence that could be used against me. I gathered my stuff to go and we snuck out of the hotel room. We didn't bother to check out at the front desk. It wasn't in my name anyway. As we walked out to the car, I couldn't help but feel strange walking next to someone that I was so close to as a teen.

"Thank you," I said as I entered the dark vehicle.

I positioned myself in a corner and began to think about the events of the night. Within minutes, I fell asleep and was jolted by a voice that no longer felt familiar to me.

"Coryn, it's time to go."

He took my hand and I exited the car and walked into the lobby being eyed by my doorman. My uneasiness was apparent. I left looking glamorous and came back looking like I was going to a football game.

"Good evening, Ms Turner."

He watched me and waited for something to happen but it didn't. My eyes told him everything was ok.

Gideon and I entered the elevator in my building and stood on opposite sides of it. The tension was thick as fog.

"Coryn, I'm sorry. I really am," He pleaded with me, but I continued to ignore him.

I took out my keys out of my clutch and fumbled with them. My hands were sweaty and shaking and couldn't put the key in the keyhole. I was nervous and him breathing down my neck didn't help. I felt his hand slip between my fingers and take the keys from me.

"Let me help," he said as he placed the key in the hole and opened the door.

"Thanks," I said as I walked inside.

When I turned around my door was still open and no one was there. I walked towards the door and peeked outside to see Gideon standing by the elevator.

"Don't you think you've already walked away from me enough in this lifetime? Might be time to actually stay and see how we can work it out!" I yelled out at him.

I couldn't hold in my anger anymore.

"Sssh it's late, and you seem distant."

Gideon walked towards my door and stepped inside. I closed the door behind him and plopped down on the couch. I was exhausted and spent. I didn't know if I was coming or going.

"Coryn, I'm sorry. I didn't lie. I just didn't tell you right away. I knew who were when we met. Our connection was natural."

"Natural? Natural? You knew how I felt about you years ago. I loved you then, but you walked away from me." I moved farther away from him as he reached out to me.

"No, YOU moved away from me. You disappeared from me when I wanted you. You were so enamored by Cass. I loved you and always wanted you. I wasn't good enough. I guess now I am, right?" He tossed the fact that I was sleeping with high-powered men in my face. That stung.

"Now the truth comes out. You knew I was a whore and wanted to sleep with me."

"I wanted to be your man. I wanted you to fall in love with me regardless of who you felt I was. The moments we spent together were to be cherished and remembered. I don't do the things I did for everyone. I knew you would enjoy it. I know you. Better than you know yourself, Coryn."

He moved closer to me and I felt his breath against my face.

"Your connection with me is manufactured. You pretended to be someone else. I liked you as Gideon. You were someone knew. I got over Bumper walking away from me, and never thought I would see you again. I loved you the moment I met you, but the day you walked away from me, you took your love with you and that's something you will have to earn again."

Bumper held me close in his arms and hugged me close. I resisted. I didn't want to be touched. With everything that was going on, I just wanted to be left alone. I was facing being called a murderer, and I just had sex with my client hours before. Surely, I couldn't have sex with my best friend.

"No. Don't. I don't want you to touch me."

I fought him off as soft kisses were placed on my flesh causing it to warm. I literally melted in his arms. He picked me up and carried me to my bedroom. Hours later, I awakened in my bed, fully clothed and Bumper was gone.

****

Six weeks had gone by and I resumed my normal behavior. As much as I wanted to quit, I couldn't. I had rent to pay. I also tried to keep a low profile. The newspapers stated that my former client Jameson Reynolds died of heart failure in a hotel room after a gala. There was no mention of a woman with him, nor was there any evidence. I was free and clear. Terrance had handled all of that.

Bumper and I spoke frequently, but nothing was the same between us. He grew to be a stranger, and it hurt my heart knowing that the one person I loved the most wouldn't be a constant in my life again. My birthday was coming up the next week, and I began to feel melancholy about life. I remembered the day I lost my mother and wondered if I would be able to love another as much as she claimed to love me. If she loved me, why would she leave me the way she did.

After some shopping, I took my purchases home and checked my AOL account to see how many appointments I had. I had been avoiding them for the last few weeks. My latest was a high-powered music mogul right here in New York. I wasn't in the mood to do any traveling so this was perfect.

I responded with a yes and got details for the event. I grabbed my red dress and heels. My hair was styled in loose curls and my make up was flawless. I was beginning to feel like myself, sexy, alluring, and irresistible. At approximately 9pm, I rode downstairs in my elevator. I checked my makeup before a white town car pulled up. The chauffeur hopped out to open the door for me and I noticed it was empty. I was the only passenger.

"Excuse me. Shouldn't there be someone else?" I said to the chauffeur.

He continued to drive, but was kind enough to calm my fears and answer my questions.

"You will meet your suitor in a few minutes," he advised.

I just sat back and waited. I've been surprised before so I was used to it.

We pulled up to the studio and I walked through the doors. The sounds of my heels clacking against the floor were the only ones I heard. Then I saw him. I recognized him immediately. My reaction said it all.

"Cass, what the fuck are you doing here?" I asked.

My palms got sweaty and I began to breathe just as heavily as I did when I was a kid. I hadn't seen him in about ten years and he still looked good. His muscles protruded through his clothing. The closer he walked to me, the more I began to panic. It was as if he glided towards me.

The room sparkled with candlelight and the music continued to play as if it were a soundtrack to our reunion. Beads of sweat appeared on my top lip, but I was too nervous to wipe it off. I don't think I blinked until the blast from my past walked right up to me, breathing my air.

"Coryn, good to see you. It's been a dream that finally turned into my reality."

He reached out to embrace me and I stiffened in his arms. I didn't know how I felt about seeing him,

147

but he always made sure to let it be known that he could buy me. I guess nothing had changed.

"Damn Cass, you didn't stop until you tried to purchase me. Are things that hard for you to get a woman to love you?" I hit him where it hurt, but it was like an elephant being hit by a fly-- no effect.

"I didn't try. You're here, right?"

He embraced me once again, and his muscles gripped me tighter than before. My pussy jumped as I smelled his cologne. This was going to be a long night.

"How did you find me, and what do you want?"

I stepped back from him and walked towards the table illuminated by candles. He followed behind me and crowded me once more, causing me to lean against a wall.

"Coryn, I always get what I want, and you have been what I wanted for years. You think because you walked away that you are out of my life? Doesn't work that way."

He grabbed my hand and placed it on his heart. I snatched my hand away and it fell to my side. He wrapped his muscular arms around me and held me close. His breath reeked of alcohol. He kissed my lips, biting my bottom one. He drew blood, and I pulled back. I tasted my DNA on my tongue, and it turned me on.

"Oh, so you wanna draw blood? Is that your way of claiming me?"

I threw my purse on the floor and pushed him away. My attempts at defending myself were futile. Cass held both hands above my head and licked my neck. His kisses lingered, and he ran his tongue across my shoulder blade. I felt instant chills. I felt myself wanting him, even though I shouldn't have.

His tongue drifted up to my cheek and licked it slowly. I shivered and he tasted my salty tears.

"Cass, tell me what the fuck you want from me!" I yelled again, but received no response.

He grabbed me and turned me around with his hand on my waist. I felt him fidgeting with my panties. There was little I could do with my face against the wall. I felt his fingers intertwine in the fabric of my lace undergarments. His fingers gripped them tightly. In one fell swoop, he ripped them off of me.

I knew a bruise would develop, but I would have to worry about that later. My face began getting marks on it from the pattern on the wall. Cass stood behind me and pulled down his pants. I heard the belt buckle hit the floor, and felt his hot body press up against mine.

"Cass, let me just talk to you for a minute. You don't have to do this."

I tried to reason with him so he wouldn't do what I knew he was doing anyway. His breath rested on my back and I felt the tip of his dick making his way towards my canal. I was slightly turned on, but the sad part was he didn't have to do this. I would have given it to him anyway.

Cass grabbed my waist and tilted me over slightly. He eased his erect dick inside of me. I gasped and I felt beads of sweat forming on my top lip. I couldn't wipe it off, and licked the salt that formed.

In and out, his chocolate covered tool drilled inside of me. I accepted it and began moaning in pleasure. That caused him to go faster and harder. Holding on to the back of my neck and pressing my face deeper into the wall, I felt him glide deep inside of me. My walls contracted, accepting him totally. I wanted him as much as he wanted me, and my body knew it. My heart still debated the issue. There was no question now.

"Fuck me. Fuck me harder, now."

My response to the drilling gave him more energy. My pussy curved to his dick, and I felt myself creaming all over it. Cass turned me around and picked me up, placing me back on his rod to ride. My hands, now free, were placed around his neck. I held on for balance as he used the wall for leverage. The muscles in his arms contracted as he lifted me up and down slowly. I kissed him slowly; my tongue lingered in his mouth. Finally, we were old enough to do all the things I wanted to do with him as a teenager.

"Do you love me?" I said to him between breaths.

My panties were thrown to the side and I had to smile. The fabric was torn and I knew I would be going commando when this was all over.

"Yes. Yes, I love you more than you know. I have always loved you, but you never gave me the chance."

Cass dove his face into my chest and bit the top of my breasts, causing me to moan. I felt my juices escape from my pussy. Where it landed, I don't know. Cass pounded my body up and down on top of his as I watched sweat drip off of his body. Needing more, he put me down so he could take his shoes and pants off. With the piano a few feet away, he picked me up and carried me over to it. My ass hit each of the keys as he strategically laid me on it so he could continue to fuck me. I wrapped my legs around his waist and I felt him go deep within me.

" Uh uh. Oh shit. Cass, I'm about to cum. Yes. Give it to me baby."

I scratched his back and neck with my fingers and dull sounds of the piano keys melodically danced off of my ass.

"Yes Coryn. Cum all over daddy's dick. Let me feel your body shiver," he said as he felt my body trembling and shivering from orgasm.

I squirted all over him and I felt his creamy fluid enter my canal. His knees grew weak and he sat on the piano bench with his head on my lap.

"Did you want this to happen? You paid for this. Is this what you paid for? Sex?"

I stroked his wavy black hair and thought about how close we were, but still yet so far. We were not in high school anymore. Life was giving us grown up shit that neither he nor I was ready for.

"I paid to see you because you kept avoiding me. You know how many times I wanted to see you and you denied my request. So I gave a fake name and had fake plans, but all this was real. I wanted to see you and be with you no matter how much it cost."

Cass looked in my eyes and I felt warm inside. His hand grazed my cheek and I caught a glimpse of a ring.

"You're married?"

I grabbed his hand and looked closely at the ring. It was a platinum diamond band. How I missed that was crazy when it was blinged out. I guess I was too focused on being in his presence to realize that he wasn't single.

"I don't love her like I loved you. You have been the only one I've loved since I was a teenager," Cass tried to rationalize things, but I wasn't having it.

I hopped off of the piano and grabbed my panties which off the floor. My shoes were tossed in a corner. I was able to retrieve them along with my purse.

"I can't believe you just had sex with me and you are married!" I yelled at him.

My face grew red with fury and I hurried towards the door. After putting his pants back on,Cass was fast on my heels. He stopped me in my tracks with his words.

"What are you bitching about? Isn't that what you get paid for?" he chuckled as he spoke those words.

I felt heat radiate through my body. I grew angry and embarrassed. I couldn't believe that was what he was throwing in my face after he was inside of me enjoying what other men pay for.

"You are absolutely fucking right! Here I am leaving when I haven't even been paid for what I've given you. Since we are friends, you get that discount. I need three thousand dollars. I want it now. It would have been five thousand, but I didn't suck your dick!"

"You dirty bitch. You aren't even worth it, but I will give you the sympathy fuck you desire."

Cass reached into his jacket that lay near the piano and took out large stacks of money. He threw it at me. Without any shame, I picked it up. I came, I saw and I delivered so I was going to take every dime that was due to me. It looked like more than what he owed me, so I placed what I could inside of my purse and walked away. I blew him a kiss as I sashayed my ass out of his studio without my panties.

"Thanks for cumming!" I said as I stepped back into reality.

I heard him call me all types of bitches, but I refused to turn back. As I grabbed a cab and made my way home, I thought about Bumper and wondered how he was. Mostly I wondered how he and I would be able to repair our broken friendship.

It had been weeks since I spoke to him and I truly missed him. The connection we built when I didn't know who he was caused me to miss him more than a little bit. I arrived at my building and tossed the taxi driver a hundred dollar bill.. Arriving at my building, I was greeted by my doorman.

"Ms. Turner, there is someone here to see you," he said, smiling at me.

He clearly had a secret, but refused to share. His smile resembled that of the Cheshire Cat. I had lived there long enough to know when he was holding a surprise. That smile was usually reserved for holidays, but today was different.

"Brandon, who is here for me? I'm not expecting any guests. I always tell you when someone is coming."

"I am not liberty to say, ma'am, but you will be very pleased. I am sure or it."

I knew that if it was someone that was a danger, he wouldn't be smiling like that so I simply nodded at him and went upstairs. As I walked into my apartment, I noticed white rose petals leading up until the door. It made me leery, but I felt a sense of peace as I turned my doorknob.

Inside, beginning from the front door and inside of my entire apartment were bouquets of white roses.

"Bumper what are you doing here? I can't believe they let you in without my permission," I said as I stepped over the bouquet of roses that were left all about my apartment. There was no corner left untouched as vases, and petals covered every inch of my path.

I removed my coat and tossed it on the back of a chair hitting some flowers causing the buds to tumble down to the floor. It was all too much for me to take in at once.

"I called and made a delivery and asked for to be let in. Money talks loudly around these parts, and I've got enough of it to make a long speech."

He walked over to me and sat me down on my white love seat. His hand wrapped around mine as he placed my hand on his face.

"Bumper, we can't keep doing this. Either we are going to be friends or lovers. I can't allow you to walk in and out of my life when it's good for you. I refuse to get my heart entangled with you when I can fall asleep and wake up to thousands of dollars that won't disappear unless I choose to spend it."

"Coryn, you can't spend the rest of your life in lust with money."

At that point, I chuckled, stood up, and began stripping in the middle of my living room floor. I removed my clothing and bent down to pick up some of the rose petals. I loved how they felt against my fingers.

To me, nothing felt better than money. I walked over to Bumper and straddled him. His erection poked me and I began grinding on top of him. His breathing grew and he buried his face inside of my chest. He touched my skin over and over, kissing areas that had already been touched by another and some that only his kisses lingered. I got him worked up, placing my hands inside of his pockets to massage him.

As I continued, I pulled out a wad of cash; hundred dollar bills mostly. I rubbed them all over my taut stomach and breasts. I tossed them over my head and they landed on me. I got up from his lap and picked up a single hundred-dollar bill that happened to land on my foot. I rubbed it slowly up my thigh and stared Bumper squarely in the eye.

I took the bill and rubbed it between my legs to absorb the moisture that emitted from it. The sweet smell was now permanently tattooed onto it. Inhaling the scent of my aroma, I leaned over and wiped the bill on his lips. Now he could taste it himself and understand just what I was coming from.

"You see that? That's me. You got me aroused, but money makes me cum."

I walked away, leaving him to his own devices and went to take a shower. I cared less that I just wiped someone else's body fluids mixed with mine unto a man that claimed to love me. I was more impressed by how much money he left me at the end of the night as opposed to how many inches he could inject me with.

"Coryn, what the fuck is wrong with you? You just wiped your pussy juice in my face. That shit isn't cool."

He wiped his face and got up to approach me in the bathroom. I had already made my way into the shower and was lathering up when I heard the door open.

"Bumper, what do you want? I have the innate ability to shut my feelings off when I need to. I'm a paid whore. It's what we get paid to do. Money fuels me. Love weakens me. The last person I loved left me."

I dropped the washcloth on the shower floor and stepped under the running water. I needed to wash away everything that happened. I wanted to start over. I don't know if I would have a chance to, but I would give it a try. Bumper stepped into the shower fully clothed and wrapped his arms around me.

"It's all for you, baby. I miss you. I love you. I want you."

He grabbed me and held me close, causing me to feel faint. This was all too much and so soon.

"What do you mean? I was so mean to you. I let you get away once again, and I didn't fight for you."

Tears began to flow from my eyes. He was the one I truly wanted and loved. He was my best friend for many years, and our bond, even after separation, would continue.

"Now that you know who I am and what I am about, let's start over. I know everything there is to know about you and even stuff you haven't told me. I just want to get to know you all over again. We can continue where we left off. No amount of money in the world is worth losing my best friend again."

His hands grazed my face and wiped the tears that escaped my eyes.

His lips found mine and his tongue parted them as we embraced in a passionate kiss. I pulled back from him when I remembered where I had been earlier in the day and what transpired. He could never know about that. He couldn't stand Cass. With the power that he had, he would turn it into an all out war. I had dealt with enough as it was and wanted some sort of peace.

My head hurt when I rolled over the morning of my birthday. All the memories I wanted to keep subdued managed to get pushed to the forefront of my brain. As Bumper slept, I rolled over and looked at him intently. He was so peaceful. His looks, at close observation hadn't changed much, so why was it so hard for me to not recognize him? I came to the conclusion that I wanted to rid myself of the past and everything that came along with it. Sadly, even those that genuinely cared for me were in the crossfire.

I threw back the covers and made my way into the living room. It was fairly early and the sun had just shone itself on my building causing rays of light to dance on my window.

As I stood in front of my window, I felt the sun beat on my face as was proof that I was alive. Many days I wanted to end it and relieve the world of my presence. I didn't because something, somewhere told me that I had a greater reason for my existence.

My sheer white nightgown framed my silhouette perfectly and I looked back towards the bedroom to see if Bumper was awake. His soft snores comforted my concerns. I walked towards a portrait I had in my living room and removed it from the wall, revealing a safe. It was where I kept my most prized possessions. I entered the combination quietly and turned the knob, opening the compartment that hid all the things from my past that I wanted to forget temporarily.

One of them was an envelope. I removed it and closed the safe doo. I sat on the couch and breathed heavily. My breath grew shallow and all I heard was the ticking of the clock on the wall. I waited all these years to open this letter. I was instructed to open it on my twenty-fifth birthday which was today. I kind of wished that I was disobedient and did it sooner, but I felt that somehow, my mother would know and something else bad would happen. Lord knows I didn't need anything else to haunt me. My past was doing wonders for my self-esteem.

I grabbed my letter opener from my center table and ran it slowly under the underside of the flap. I didn't know what secret this would entail, but there was no stopping now. I unraveled the sheets of paper and began reading.

167

Coryn,

Happy Birthday.

If you are reading this on your birthday, thank you for waiting until you were mature to digest all I'm about to tell you. First off, I wanted to say I'm sorry. I know you expected more from me as your mother, but I couldn't keep living a lie anymore. Please remember that what I'm about to tell you is for your own good and it's why you have become who you are.

I am not your mother. I am your father's second cousin. Your mother was married to your father, but he kept cheating on her- specifically with me. She grew very angry that he and I were in love, despite the fact that we were related, in a sense. Her anger grew when she discovered I was pregnant. She also became pregnant by him months later.

When I discovered that he was still sleeping with her, I was very depressed. I never ate, or slept and wanted him to be miserable. He was and promised to still be there for me. When your mother found out, she grew angry and we fought everyday; sometimes physically. One day we went to the extreme and the physical altercation caused me to miscarry the baby. She was determined to make sure she was the only one to carry the Turner name. Her feelings were mixed.

One day while at home she had a stroke and died while experiencing preterm labor. I found her and called your father. He was heartbroken, but we promised to keep a secret. Since everyone knew I was pregnant, and I was very quiet, we decided to maintain that I would be your mother and raise you. I'm sorry you had to find out this way. I'm also sorry that your father didn't love me enough and honor me even though I was the one that made the sacrifice. You are not the only child though. You have a sister. I don't know where she is, but she's younger than you by six years. Find her and reconcile. She's the only tie you have to your father. The day before your father died, he revealed that he got someone else pregnant. That was why I hated him so much. I know this is a lot, but this is why I had to go. I loved you more than life itself, especially since you belonged to him. I loved him as a matter of fact, despite the fact that you belonged to him. However, I will always be your momma. Please forgive me. Happy Birthday.

I love you.

Tears flowed freely from my face and landed on the paper. My face, as brown as it was, felt flushed and heat radiated to it. The anger I felt welled up in me. Before I knew it, I walked into my kitchen for a glass of water. I needed to cool down. I needed to relax before I met my fate and collapsed of heart failure. I was angry because my father died without telling me. I was angry because the woman I called my mother wasn't related to me at all.

I poured out some water and drank it. I refilled the glass and placed it on the counter. It was filled halfway. A pessimist would say it was half-empty. An optimist would say it was half-full. Nonetheless, it represented how I felt at this time- transparent and unsure. I had no idea what to do and where to begin to find this girl.

Did she look like me? Was she even in New York? Have I seen her before? I decided that I had too many questions and no definite answers. My anger filled up and there was no outlet so I threw the glass filled with water against the wall. Water splashed everywhere and I collapsed in a heap on the kitchen floor. The sounds of glass shattering woke up Bumper and he came running to me.

"Coryn! What is that? Are you okay?" he said when he reached the living room.

I began to cry and my sobbing caused him to find me. Shards of glass were everywhere and he stepped over them carefully.

"A lie! My life is a lie! Everything is a lie. I am not who I say I am," I cried into his shoulder.

Bumper held me close and lovingly stroked my hair. He cradled me in his arms and carried me into the bedroom. I cried myself to sleep as he held me. There was nothing else to be said. He loved me no matter who I was or what I did. He asked no questions, and his actions gave plenty of answers.

Living a Lie

A few hours later, I woke up and Bumper had already cleaned up the living room. No evidence of glass or water remained. All my flowers that he gave to me the night before were arranged as neatly as possible on every table and area that would hold them. He was freshly dressed in a pair of wheat Timberland boots, Levi's jeans and a hoodie. I wrapped my robe around me and brushed stray hairs out of my hair.

"Rise and shine! I took the liberty of cleaning up and making some coffee. Go grab some sweats and come on back. We've got a full day ahead of us," he said with so much enthusiasm I could vomit.

My day and my life had drastically changed and he wanted us to go out?

"No, I'm not feeling up to it. Besides as young as I am, I feel like I've lived the life of someone twice my age." I quipped.

It was true. I felt like all my life has been lived up until a few hours prior and I had nothing else to look forward to.

"You actually have a new lease on life, Coryn. Now go get dressed. You and I will paint the town whatever color you choose."

"Black. I want it to be black to match my mood," I said staring blankly into his eyes. I meant every word.

"So it shall be," Bumper nodded and waited for me to come back.

As I stood in the bathroom, I washed my face and brushed my teeth. As I brushed my tongue, a wave of nausea rushed over me. The empty contents of my stomach released itself into my sink.

Bumper rushed into the bathroom and saw me collapsed onto the floor. I could no longer contain myself. The cold linoleum comforted me as I began to feel hot flashes. I literally hugged the toilet bowl. It was then that I realized that I could possibly be pregnant. I had a feeling whose it was, but it could be anyone's, given my line of work.

"When were you going to tell me?" he asked as he brought me a glass of ginger ale and some crackers. I looked up at him and another wave of nausea took over my body.

"There's nothing to tell. If I knew beforehand, I still wouldn't tell you. It's none of your business anyway."

I took a sip of the ginger ale and immediately brought it back up. My body alternated between feeling hot and feeling cold. I didn't know what I was going to do. I wasn't ready to be a mother. That much I knew for sure.

"So you mean to tell me that you wouldn't tell me that you were pregnant even if you knew beforehand?" He took a seat on the side of the bathtub listening intently to my answer.

"No. You would never know. Remember you came into my life very recently. Everything I did before you just recently came into my life was of my own hand. I worked hard and accomplished things without you. I had no one. I still have no one...."

Bumper looked at me and held his head down in his hands. He looked defeated, and my smug attitude wasn't helping. How would I fare having a baby without the father?

"I love you enough to raise this baby because it's a part of you. Anything that comes from you is god-sent and I want to be a part of it."

Bumper held me gently under my armpit and lifted me up to get me upright. He helped me into the shower and I took a quick one. He grabbed my towel and wrapped it around my body.

As much as he wanted to make love to me, he decided against it. I saw the way he looked at me and I at him, we decided to just chill. I grabbed my hoodie and sweatpants and threw my hair in a ponytail. I had absolutely no color, but added some colored lipgloss so I could put some color in my face.

"Where are we going?" I asked as I stepped unto the sidewalk. The ride downstairs was silent for the most part. Nausea had subsided and I just wanted something to eat.

"We are going to spend the day in the city as tourists. Today is your birthday and you really haven't celebrated."

He stood holding me close and staring into my eyes. "Where do you want to go for your birthday? I will take you anywhere you want."

Unfortunately I was absent of feeling on a day that was celebratory of when I entered the world. Instead of confetti and glitter, I felt like darkness followed me wherever I went. In a matter of minutes, my life had changed.

"The abortion clinic," I stated blankly.

Life or Death

"Coryn, you can't be serious!"

My face resembled a statue. I was serious and void of emotion. I wanted this thing out of me. It would cause me just as much of a problem as I was to everyone else. I couldn't bear to be the cause behind the misery of the world. I had enough of my own.

Bumper released my hands and his arms fell to his sides. He was shocked. I was tired.

"I am very serious. Then I want to go to sleep. I am not hungry. I am fed up. Nothing that I wanted to go right has. My life has been filled with drama since the moment I was born. Why would I want to subject someone else to that?"

"I will help you raise it. Please don't do this. If you feel no one loves you, remember that I do."

"Do you? Or do you just love who you believed I was and what you could do for me. You know I do everything on my own. You are the type of man that loves rescuing women. Always been. Now I saved myself. I don't need you."

I turned and began to walk away from him when he spoke words that pierced my heart instantly.

"It's not about who you need or want. Love is about who needs and wants you."

I stopped and looked at him. I couldn't even cry. It was what I needed to hear. I slowly walked back and put my hand in his intertwining our fingers. I found who I was looking for. What I didn't know was someone was looking for me and they were going to throw a monkey wrench in my plans to be happy.

A few months later, my baby bump began to protrude and I got those tiny kicks that one feels in their early months. Bumper wasn't kidding. He was there for me just like he promised. He brought me ginger ale and crackers and we redecorated my apartment. He bought a condo in my building for the hell of it, but spent the most time with me. I guess when you have money like that, that's what you do.

My bills were still paid for. My business ceased. I can't lie- I miss the glitz and glamour, but I also craved what a family was all about. Bumper gave me the love and affection that I needed and wanted.

One day, as I sat at home watching television, I was tempted to go back to the life I once knew. I was flipping through some baby books trying to figure out a name when my doorbell rang.

"Who is it? Bumper? Baby, did you leave something?" I asked through the door.

He had left about thirty minutes ago and stated he would be back in a little while. I looked through the peephole and saw the back of a head. Thinking it was him, I unlatched the lock and opened the door. To my surprise, it was Cass...my past ready to stir up trouble.

"Why hello there." he said, sounding charming as ever.

The weather had changed and the heat was never below eighty degrees. I was wearing one of Bumper's Hanes t-shirts and a pair of leggings. My Reebok Classics rest comfortably on my feet. My hair was curled lightly and I wore just a hint of lip-gloss. I definitely had a pregnancy glow.

"Cass, what the hell are you doing here? How did you find out where I lived?"

I was curious because the last time we saw each other we were at each other's throats.

"I came here to apologize as a matter of fact. I emailed you, but got no response. I called, but you never answered. I texted, but you never called me back. I figured the next best thing, and to show sincerity, was to just come to Mohammed since Mohammed never left the mountain."

"I disabled my email, changed my number, and tossed my two way. I don't need anyone interfering in what I am creating now."

I rubbed my tummy lovingly. It took a while, but I was getting used to this pregnancy thing.

"Well, I see you have already created something. When are you due?" he asked cocking his head to the side.

"I am due in about five months, and no, it's not yours." I answered the question that I knew was burning within him.

"Oh ok, well tell my man congrats on his seed. Didn't know he had it in him." Cass said sarcastically.

"It's not his, but I will share the news with him."

As soon as I said those words, I regretted it. Cass smirked and my mouth dropped. Stepping right behind him was Bumper who heard me say the baby wasn't his. Even though the baby wasn't his, it wasn't public knowledge. He loved me and the baby and would love it just as if it was his own seed. For me to verbalize it was a slap in the face to him.

"Hey, Coryn. I left my phone."

Bumper brushed past me to get his phone that was on the island in the kitchen. I didn't hear any of the vibrations indicating he was getting messages.

"Hi Baby," I said barely above a whisper. He kissed me on the cheek, glaring at me in the process.

"I will see you later okay?" I said trying to soften the mood. He never responded.

Cass stood at the door and stared at me as I looked uncomfortably at the ground. I counted each tile on the floor that I stood in about a dozen times. I hated when my mouth got me in trouble.

"So he mad with you that I'm here or that you told the truth?" Cass interrogated.

"Both. Why don't you tell me the reason why you are here so you can get off my welcome mat because you stepping on it isn't doing any justice at all."

I refused to allow him in my apartment. Nothing good had come from him standing outside for minutes, so for him being inside would cause nothing but chaos.

At his side, I noticed that he held some flowers along with an envelope. I hadn't noticed it before. I'm sure that added to Bumper's aggravation.

"These are for you. I wanted to apologize for how we left things. I was rude, obnoxious, and disrespectful. I was a brat that acted like he didn't get his favorite toy. I always wanted you, but never knew how to speak before. Now that I had you, I want more."

I cocked my head at that response. "Cass, there's no more to get. You paid for it. I spent it. You won't be getting it back. That's all there is to it. Ask your wife to give it to you."

"She was in a car accident three months before you and I got together. She was the one that told me to find you and link up. Bree knew she couldn't satisfy me the way I needed. We always talked about you. She knew how I felt from when we were in school."

The name rang a bell. I remember her being one of the girls from school that fought for him on one particular day. Funny how we get what we want and still want more.

"Cass, I'm sorry about everything that has happened while we lost contact, but as you can see, I am very pregnant, very committed, and very busy. My time is no longer available to you."

I quietly closed the door and left him standing there. I had enough drama for the day and I didn't want to incite any more problems later on when Bumper came home.

When Bumper came home hours later, he found me asleep on his side of the bed. I often did that to be sure that he would wake me up when he got in. If not, he would let me sleep forever and I would have no clue where he was or where he was going.

I heard him shuffling around the room and it caused me to stir. I rolled over and looked at his back as he sat down on the bed. His hands were clasped in front of him and his brows were furrowed in the reflection I spotted in the mirror.

"Bumper, what's wrong?" I placed my hand on his lower back and he moved.

He had never reacted that way with me before. I removed my palm and used it to push myself up. I knew what this was about. If this wasn't fixed, we would continue to have issues.

"Coryn, go back to sleep," he said with no emotion.

He took off his watch and placed it on the nightstand. His wallet lay there along with an envelope. I dared to see what it was, but I decided against it.

"I'm not sleepy anymore. Baby, please tell me what's wrong! I apologize for what I said earlier. I didn't mean to say it, and I damn sure didn't mean for you to hear it. You know it took me a while to adjust to this life. I'm still unsure how I'm going to manage."

I threw my legs over the edge of the end and walked around to join him.

"It's cool. Don't worry. Let's not talk about it anymore."

He got up to walk away but I stopped him.

"No, we have to talk about it. No, this is not biologically your child, but it will call you daddy. Thankfully, because of your friend, we won't have to worry about who the daddy is and it will be all yours."

Bumper reached over and handed me the envelope.

""What's this?" I asked as I opened the flap.

I received no response. Clearly, I would have to figure it out on my own.

As I opened the envelope, my heart sunk. It was a subpoena. The wife of Jameson Reynolds was forcing me to get a paternity test for my unborn child. If the baby was her husband's then she wanted custody.

Bumper had nothing to say. I didn't either. My decision was either have the baby and have it taken away or abort it and avoid being a mother to a child I didn't really want anyway.

Flesh of my Flesh

As the months passed, my bump did also. My patience grew weary as Bumper and I grew closer. I loved him and he loved me. We were working on building a life. Unfortunately, our life was not panning out the way we needed it to be. Things got relatively worse at a routine doctor appointment.

"Bumper, can you not walk so fast? You know I waddle when I walk now."

I reached out my hand and tried to keep up to my boyfriend. He took it and matched my stride as we took the walk down Broadway to the doctor's office. I was eight months, and it was time to see if we were having a boy or a girl. We decided late that we wanted to find out what it would be so we could finish shopping.

"Are you excited to know what we are having?" he said as we entered the lobby and pushed the elevator to the building.

I loved the fact that he said 'we.' After the situation with Cass, and the fact that I let slip that the baby wasn't biologically his, he didn't mention it often. I was happy to know that he still loved the baby as if it was his own.

Even though Congressman Reynolds' wife threatened to take the baby when it was born if a paternity test determined that her husband was the father, I decided to keep it anyway. It was mine. I had never had anything that belonged to me before. Even my virtue belonged to someone else. It was time that I had something for myself.

"Yeah, I actually am. I've been sending my personal assistant to get baby clothes while I'm in the studio. We should be done with the nursery in a few weeks."

We arrived and he took my coat to hang it up on the coat rack. I sat and picked up the latest Parent's Magazine while he checked his pager for messages. I looked at him affectionately.

"I was thinking Natasha for a girl and Shane for a boy. What do you think?" I asked Bumper, but he was too into watching some nurses and doctors speak in a hushed whisper.

I tried to get his attention but he was intently watching them as they pointed and looked at us in a way that even made me uncomfortable. I ignored them and paid more attention to Bumper.

"Yeah baby, I like that a lot. I want my first name to be his middle name and your first name to be her middle name. It's only right. That's our connection to them."

He squeezed my hand and smiled then placed his hand on my stomach and at that moment felt a tiny kick in his palm. We kissed and were interrupted by my name being called.

"Turner...Coryn Turner. The doctor is ready for you," she said as she wrote some notes on my clipboard.

Bumper grabbed my hand and guided me into the room. I waddled slowly and stepped up onto the exam table.

"Hi. I am Marissa and I am your nurse for the day. Dr. Bacchus will be with you shortly. Let me take your vitals."

She placed the blood pressure cuff around my arm and inserted the stems of the stethoscope into her ears. She listened intently for my beats. I grew nervous because Dr. Bacchus wasn't my regular doctor. I looked nervously at Bumper.

"Ma'am, what happened to Dr. Weaver? He's the only one that I have ever dealt with, and he's the one scheduled to deliver my baby."

"Our baby," Bumper corrected me.

He smiled at me and I halfheartedly returned it. There was something uneasy about what was happening, but I couldn't put my finger on it.

I looked at Bumper and he gave me an uneasy smile, but a smile nonetheless. The nurse removed the blood pressure cuff and hand me a gown to change into. As much as I didn't want to, I decided to try to relax and let things happen.

"Sir, can you please leave so we can begin examining your wife. The doctor doesn't want anyone in the room who isn't a nurse or doctor. We will call you when she's ready."

The nurse held the door open for him to leave, but he stood right there.

"This is my baby too, and I want to know the progress."

Bumper stood by my side, refusing to leave the room. I gripped his hand tightly and tears began to well up out of nervousness.

"Why can't he stay?" I asked but my question fell on deaf ears.

"He has to leave now."

She slammed the door behind her and waited for me to say goodbye. I reluctantly kissed him and he wiped my tears.

"It will be okay. I promise. I love you. I will be right in the hallway waiting for you."

He kissed my lips slowly and walked out of the room, closing the door behind him. The silence of the room was overwhelming. The smell of the office was sterile and ammonia overpowered me. I stripped down to my underwear and put on the nightgown I was given. I lay on the exam table and waited for someone to come.

"Ms Turner, it's good to see you. I am your doctor for the day. Dr. Weaver is busy with another patient. You know how it is. Babies are so demanding. Why don't you lay back so we can set you up?"

Dr. Bacchus held my hand, but I pulled back. It was cold and uninviting. I received a stern glare but didn't care. I was uncomfortable and I let my feelings show. I didn't know this person at all. This wasn't my regular doctor. My hands were clammy and cool due to being nervous. Aside from my moving baby, there were bouts of nervousness happening within.

Marissa, the nurse assisting, came in and began getting items prepared to give me an IV. She also pulled a sonogram machine into the room. I watched as she hooked me up to the machine so I would be able to see my baby. She placed the leads on various parts of my stomach. I got excited as she placed jelly on my stomach and the wand to locate my child. Once focused, the machine allowed me the ability to see fingers, toes. and even hear the heartbeat.

"Would you like to know what it is?."

"Yes I would like to know. I always wanted a son."

The nurse focused the wand on one particular spot and directed my attention to the screen. The baby kept moving around. I felt chills as she touched my stomach. Something wasn't right, but I couldn't place it. Finally, my baby stopped moving long enough for her to decipher the gender.

"Well, look here! Our prayers have been answered," the technician smiled with a glisten in her eye.

She seemed to be more excited than I was. She took a piece of cloth and wiped off my belly as I lay back smiling. I closed my eyes with that wonderful vision of my son in my stomach, but was interrupted by a tiny prick in my arm.

"What's going on? What's that for?"

My tongue began to feel as dry as sandpaper and thick as a cement block. My consciousness was diminishing rapidly, and everything in the room was getting blurry.

"It's just a little something for the tiny procedure we are about to have. Don't worry. When we are all done, you will be just like a new woman. It will be like you were never pregnant."

I felt a burning sensation within my veins and my head was being lifted up. I saw colorful spots of yellow, red, and green. My eyes felt heavy, and my face felt like someone was sitting on it. My words were slurred and slow.

"I........ want........... my .... baby........."

I struggled to get that simple sentence out of my mouth. I swallowed and the rest of my voice was stuck in my throat. My eyes grew heavy and tired. Everything around me grew black and blurry. My body felt heavy and I could no longer see.

The last thing I felt was cold steel against my stomach. I felt pulling and tugging as my baby was being ripped from its nest within my body. The one thing that I decided I wanted was about to be gone too. My subconscious knew more than my conscious and somehow, someway... someone would have to PAY!

To Be Continued.........

Other novels by our authors
from Peach Dollhouse

Peach Dollhouse (A Sugar Babies Series)

To Love, Honor and Betray

Young Lady

Young Lady 2

Nothing was the Same

Heavy in the Game

I Will Always Love You

I Will Always Love You 2

Allergic To Loyalty

Allergic to Loyalty 2

Doll Squad

Straight from the Gutta 1-3

Paid Dues

Same Script, Different Cast

Made in the USA
Middletown, DE
07 August 2022